THE DO-OVER

THE DO-OVER

OVER

JENNIFER HONEYBOURN

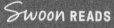

Swoon Reads
New York

A Swoon Reads Book

An imprint of Feiwel and Friends and Macmillan Publishing Group, LLC

120 Broadway, New York, NY 10271

Our books may be purchased in bulk for promotional, educational, or business
use. Please contact your local bookseller or the Macmillan Corporate and
Premium Sales Department at (800) 221-7945 ext. 5442 or by email at
MacmillanSpecialMarkets@macmillan.com.

Library of Congress Control Number: 2019948822

ISBN 978-1-250-19468-8 (hardcover) / ISBN 978-1-250-19469-5 (ebook)

Book design by Trisha Previte

First edition, 2020

10 9 8 7 6 5 4 3 2 1

swoonreads.com

FOR TONY

THE DO-OVER

✳ CHAPTER ✳
1

"You know, it's not too late to back out," Alistair says. His mom's minivan's still running, and he's squeezing the steering wheel like he's prepared to peel out of Ben's street just as soon as I give the word.

"Why would we want to back out?" My hands are shaking as I pull down the passenger-side mirror to check my lip gloss. Yup, still just as glossy as they were five minutes ago when I last checked.

"The question you should be asking is why you want to hang out with Ben Griffin in the first place," Alistair mumbles.

"Be nice," Marisol warns him from the back seat.

"I'm always nice," he says.

I give him the side-eye.

"Most of the time." He sighs heavily and turns off the van. He pulls a black beanie over his dark hair, which is shaved on the sides, long and curly on top, like an English sheepdog, and always falling into his gray eyes.

He looks hot, even if he is wearing his weird fingerless black leather gloves.

Stop it, I think, my cheeks flushing. He's not hot. He's Alistair.

The three of us climb out of the van and walk down the street. It's snowing lightly, and quite a few of the surrounding houses still have their holiday lights up, even though we're already well into January. With every step toward Ben's house, my heart starts to race faster. Ben and his crowd are in a completely different social stratosphere from me and my friends, and maybe it's shallow and silly, but being liked by them—and especially by Ben—matters to me. Way more than it probably should.

I still can't believe he invited us over. Well, me. Ben invited *me* over. And I brought my two best friends with me, because no way was I showing up to Ben Griffin's house alone.

"Bonus Round is still open for another hour," Alistair says, tugging on the collar of his tattered jean jacket as we head up Ben's snow-covered driveway. Bonus Round is the game-themed café where you can usually find us on the weekend, playing Settlers of Catan for hours on end. "Just throwing that out there."

Marisol shakes her head. "Stop. This is going to be fun."

Alistair snorts. "I don't think there is any fun to be had around Ben Griffin and his idiot jock friends. Not unless you're into beer pong or breaking people's spirits. Which, it goes without saying, I am not."

"Come on, Al. They're not that bad," she says.

He stares at her, his thick eyebrows drawing together. "Raise your hand if you've ever been personally victimized by Ben

Griffin." His hand shoots high into the air. Marisol shoots me a guilty look and raises her hand, too.

"Well, middle school was a long time ago," I say. "He's changed." Lab Partner Ben is a definite upgrade from Middle School Ben. He's Ben 2.0. Sweeter and funnier, not to mention unbelievably good-looking. And, okay, I know that looks aren't everything, but I can't fight the pheromones.

"Guys like that don't change," Alistair scoffs. "They just learn how to hide their Neanderthal-ness a little better." He pulls a pack of cigarettes out of the front pocket of his jean jacket. *Candy* cigarettes. He shakes one of the thin white candy sticks out of the pack, taps the stick against the pack, and then puts it to his mouth, where it dangles from his lips as if it's a real cigarette.

I narrow my eyes. I know what he's doing—he's planning to act as weird as possible in front of Ben and his friends, thereby ensuring that we'll never be asked to another party, ever again. Alistair is going to blow my chance at getting to know them better.

"Quit. It." I grab the pack from him and stuff it in the pocket of my puffy jacket before ringing the doorbell.

"I cannot believe we're doing this," Alistair murmurs. "We're about to willingly walk into enemy territory."

"They're not our enemies—" I say, just as the door swings open.

Olivia Brandt is standing in front of us, tall and blond and basically flawless. I feel like a garden gnome whenever I'm around her.

"Um, hi. Is Ben home?" I ask.

My face burns. Stupid question. Of course he's home. He lives here.

Olivia's eyes narrow. I can tell she's thinking about denying us entry, but after a long moment she smiles tightly and steps back to let us inside.

"Olympia, right?" Alistair asks her as we enter the house.

I shoot him a dirty look. He knows her name—we've all gone to school together since kindergarten.

"Olivia, actually," she says. "Albert, right?"

Alistair gives her a wide smile and pretends to puff on his candy cigarette. Olivia rolls her eyes and leaves us in the hall to fend for ourselves.

"Well, we're off to a fine start," he says.

Marisol pokes him in the arm. "Why couldn't you just say hello?"

He frowns. "Wait, are you taking her side?"

"There are no sides," I say, shrugging off my coat. "We're all friends here."

"Are we, though?"

I ignore him.

Alistair glances around, taking in the black-and-white checkerboard floor, the vaulted ceiling, the massive crystal chandelier. "Why do good houses happen to bad people?"

I shake my head. I get that he doesn't like Ben, and, okay, yes, Ben hasn't been all that nice to Alistair over the years, so maybe his feelings are sort of justified—but that was years ago. We've all grown up since then. I wish that Alistair would just forgive and forget and give Ben a second chance.

I shrug out of my puffy jacket. Alistair gapes at me, a flush rising in his cheeks.

"What?"

"Nothing." He clears his throat. "It's just that you don't usually wear . . . stuff like that."

By *stuff like that*, he obviously means clothes that hint that I actually have a body. Normally, I'm in oversized T-shirts and jeans, but tonight I opted for something a bit more fashion-forward, to give me a fighting chance at fitting in with this crowd.

"You look great, Em," Marisol says, pushing her thick, black-framed glasses up the bridge of her ski-jump nose. Her mass of dark, curly hair is tamed into a ponytail, and she's wearing a red chenille sweater that I've never seen before. So maybe I'm not the only one worried about fitting in.

"What she said," Alistair murmurs.

"Thanks."

I toss my jacket on top of the pile of coats on the stairs. Marisol's Doc Marten boots squeak against the marble floor as we follow the sound of laughter down the hall and into the kitchen. I fiddle with the leather friendship bracelet she gave me last Christmas, a pit in my stomach. Walking into the middle of a party is super awkward, especially when I'm not totally sure what kind of reception we're going to get. Ben may have asked me to come, but I'm not sure his friends will be too thrilled to see us. Olivia certainly didn't seem to be.

Ben invited me, I remind myself. *I belong here.*

Ben's kitchen is crammed with people. The entire basketball

team is here, along with the cheerleading squad and a few other kids I don't recognize. Most people are either sitting at the long wooden farm table playing quarters, or in the adjoining room, watching a boxing match on the big-screen TV.

No one even notices us—so, no different from school, then.

Alistair, Marisol, and I stand at the edge of the room. I glance anxiously around, but I don't see Ben anywhere. I do see Camila Nunes, captain of the cheerleading squad and Ben's most recent ex-girlfriend, perched on the marble-topped island, surrounded by pizza boxes and half-empty bottles of liquor. Her long dark hair is stylishly messy, like she just rolled out of bed. She's all bee-stung lips and legs for miles, the girl at the top of the cheer pyramid looking down at the rest of us.

My breath catches as I realize she's wearing Ben's basketball jersey.

Oh God, they're back together. I've totally misread Ben and he just wants to be friends. What was I thinking, coming here?

But before I can tell Alistair and Marisol that I've made a huge mistake and changed my mind and we need to leave *right now*, I spot Ben weaving through the crowd of our drunken classmates toward us. His blond hair is adorably rumpled, and he's smiling at me in a way that immediately calms my nerves and makes me forget all about the fact that Camila is wearing his jersey. There's definitely something behind that smile of his—something more than just friendship.

I know it.

"Emelia! You came." Ben wraps his arms around me and lifts me off my feet. I flush at the unexpected closeness, the way our bodies are pressed so tightly together. Everyone who wasn't looking in my direction before is definitely looking now, including Camila, and I don't hate the feeling.

Ben sets me back down. He notices Marisol and Alistair and his smile falters for a second, but then he recovers and turns the full wattage of his game show–host grin on them.

"Hey, good to see you," he says.

"Thanks for inviting us," Marisol says, bouncing slightly.

Ben's eyes flick to me and I hold my breath.

"Yeah, of course," he says.

"I'm just here for the gasoline," Alistair says.

Ben's brow furrows in confusion. "What?"

"*Mad Max Two*. Ever seen it?"

"Nope."

"I'm not surpri—"

I laugh and punch Alistair hard in the shoulder. "Don't mind him. He has this weird habit of quoting movies." Alistair wants to be a director someday, so we watch a lot of movies together. For some reason, dialogue seems to stick in his brain.

Alistair frowns and rubs his shoulder as Ben offers us something to drink.

"Olivia made some vodka punch," he says. "I should warn you, though, it's pretty strong."

"I'm in," I say.

"Are you sure, Em?" Marisol says. "Remember what happened the last time you drank—"

I cut her off with a look. Why are my friends so determined to embarrass me? Ben does not need to know that I once got drunk on wine coolers and spent the entire night trying to throw up as quietly as possible so my parents wouldn't hear.

Marisol gets the message. "I mean, vodka punch sounds great," she says.

Ben leads us over to the punch bowl, which happens to be beside Camila. She watches us approach with narrowed eyes, fiddling with the star charm that hangs from a gold chain around her neck.

"Hey," she says to Alistair. "Weren't you in my Spanish class last semester?"

Alistair gives her a lazy smile. *"Sí."*

"I remember you," she says.

"Yo también te recuerdo. Apestas en español," he replies.

Loose translation: I remember you, too. You suck at Spanish.

Camila leans forward and grabs Alistair's collar, drawing him toward her. *"Ya no apesto. No en español ni ninguna otra cosa."*

I don't suck anymore. Not at Spanish, and not at anything else.

She closes the last few inches of space between them and suddenly they're kissing. She's kissing Alistair and he's not pushing her away! In fact, from the way his arm slides around her waist, those ridiculous fingerless gloves clutching her back, he seems to be enjoying it.

Marisol smothers a laugh, but I don't think there's anything funny about this. My chest burns. I mean, Alistair and I are just friends; he's free to kiss whoever he wants. I should be happy—after all, this clearly means that Ben and Camila aren't back together. And Ben is the one I'm here for.

So why, then, do I want to yank Alistair away from her?

When Camila finally lets him go, she glances at Ben and I realize with some relief that this is all just a show to make him jealous. Only it doesn't seem to be working. Ben calmly ladles vodka punch into a red Solo cup for me, completely unbothered that his ex just kissed someone else right in front of him.

I wish I was unbothered.

I can feel Alistair staring at me, but I don't meet his gaze.

He clears his throat. *"Definitivamente no apestas en eso,"* he says to Camila.

You definitely don't suck at that.

I shake my head, trying to douse the little ember of jealousy inside me.

Ben hands me the Solo cup and I knock the vodka punch back. I drink it so fast that I start to cough.

"Whoa," Ben says, rubbing my back. "Take it easy. I told you, it's strong."

But I'm glad that it's strong, and I don't want to take it easy. I want to scrub what I just saw from my memory. I want to do something that will make me forget about Alistair and Camila. I want to forget about everything except Ben.

I set the empty cup down hard on the counter and glare at Alistair.

You want to know who else doesn't suck at kissing, Alistair Stewart?

Spoiler alert: It's me! I don't suck at it. In fact, I'm fairly excellent at it. As Ben is about to find out.

I grab Ben's hand and drag him out of the kitchen, away from everyone, but especially Alistair and Camila. A cheer goes up from the great room as whoever it is that's fighting in the boxing match goes down for the count.

"Where are we going?" Ben asks.

"I don't know." I just wanted to get away; I didn't think about where we were going. I haven't ever been inside his house before, so I don't even know which direction to take.

Ben chuckles. "Come on."

He leads me down the hall, and the sound of the party fades as we enter a dark room that feels several degrees cooler than the rest of the house. He plugs in a string of tiny lanterns that hang suspended from the ceiling, casting dim, soft light on a room made entirely of windows.

"This is my favorite place," he says.

"I can see why." Outside, snow swirls against the dark velvet of the sky. A crescent moon peeks through the clouds, glinting off the dark river that twists through the evergreen trees in his backyard.

Ben grabs a velvety gray blanket from the arm of the wicker couch. He sits down and shakes the blanket over his legs, then holds the corner up, an invitation for me to slip in beside him.

My heart is about to pound right out of my chest. I didn't really think this through, and now that we're alone, I'm not sure what to do. I want to kiss him—obviously, I want to kiss him. I've been dreaming about this moment for longer than I care to admit.

I'm shaking as I walk over and sit down beside him.

"I'm glad you came tonight," Ben says as we huddle under the blanket. "I wasn't sure you would."

"Really? Why?"

"I don't know. I guess I don't know how to read you. And you're kind of intimidating."

Wait, he thinks I'm intimidating? Mind. Blown. Until we started talking in science class a few weeks ago, Ben Griffin seemed as far away and as impossibly out of reach as a star. And even though I know him a little better now, it still kind of feels that way.

He reaches over and gently twists a strand of my long red hair around his finger. The thought that he might be nervous is way too much for my brain to take in.

"Your hair is awesome," he says. "It looks just like a sunset."

And, okay, it's kind of a corny thing to say, but maybe I like corny. Maybe it doesn't always have to be clever banter.

I swallow. "Thanks."

His blue eyes lock on mine. He slides his arm around the back of the couch, and then slides a little closer to me, and we're kissing and *oh my God*, I can't believe this is happening.

Ben Griffin is kissing me. And I'm kissing him back! I am kissing Ben Griffin and he is kissing me and I'm pretty sure that I'm going to spontaneously combust.

For one second, Alistair and his lopsided smile hijack my thoughts and I wonder what it would be like to be on this couch with him instead, but I quickly push the image away. He probably has his hand up Camila's shirt by now.

And speaking of hands up shirts . . .

Ben's fingers are warm against my lower back. He stops kissing my mouth and moves to my neck. Somehow, I find myself lying on the couch, Ben stretched out on top of me. I'm so lost in my feelings, so lost in Ben, that I don't realize we're not alone until someone clears their throat.

Ben jumps off me. His blond hair is sticking up in all directions, his T-shirt is wrinkled, and he's breathing hard.

Alistair's standing in the doorway, arms crossed, his face all hard angles. "Marisol's not feeling well. I'm taking her home. You coming?"

I sit up, tugging my sweater down so that it covers my stomach. My head is spinning. I'm not sure if I'm light-headed from the vodka punch or from kissing Ben.

"I'll make sure she gets home," Ben says.

"That's okay," Alistair says. "I brought her, so I can take her—"

"No, it's fine," I interrupt him. "I'm going to stay a bit longer."

He frowns. "Are you sure that's a good idea?"

This is the second time tonight one of my friends has questioned my judgment, and honestly, it's super annoying. "Yes, I'm sure," I snap.

Alistair scowls. "Fine, whatever." He turns on his heel and leaves.

"Wow, he really doesn't like me," Ben says.

I shake my head. "He really doesn't."

He laughs and laces his fingers through mine. "Well, I guess that's fair enough. I was kind of a dick to him when we were kids."

I like that he's acknowledging that he treated Alistair unfairly in middle school. I just wish Alistair had stuck around to hear it. Maybe it would make a difference to know that Ben is sorry.

"So." Ben runs his thumb lightly over the back of my hand. "Winter formal is coming up. I was wondering if you'd go with me."

I stare at him and the world stops. Ben Griffin is asking me to winter formal. Ben Griffin, captain of the basketball team, hottest guy in school, is asking me to winter formal. Me! To winter formal!

I can't keep the smile off my face. "I'd love to."

"Perfect." He leans over and kisses the tip of my nose. "It's a date."

We make out some more, Ben's hands tangled in my hair, my fingers moving without direction, the just-barely-there scruff on his cheeks burning my skin, until I'm dangerously close to curfew. Ben runs upstairs to his room to grab his keys so he can take me home. I head back into the kitchen and find Alistair by himself at the table, building a pyramid of Solo cups. Everyone else has migrated to the great room.

"You're still here," I say.

He shrugs. "I came back after I took Marisol home."

"I told you Ben would drive me. You didn't have to come back."

"Yes, I did." He places a cup at the very top of the pyramid. It wobbles for a moment before toppling over, bringing all the cups crashing to the floor. "Drinking and driving don't mix. That's why I ride a bike."

I stare at him, confused.

"*Pretty in Pink*?" he says.

I roll my eyes. "Not everyone has every movie they've ever watched memorized."

Alistair sighs. "What are we doing here, Em?"

"What do you mean?"

"You know what I mean," he says, bending down to collect the cups. "Since when do you care about anyone in this crowd? Just look around. We don't fit in here."

Maybe he doesn't fit in, but I could. Ben asking me to winter formal is proof that I belong. I could be part of the popular crowd.

"You didn't seem worried about that when you were kissing Camila," I point out.

"She kissed me."

"You didn't stop her."

His lips quirk.

"You aren't even trying to talk to anyone," I say. He could have joined everyone else in the other room. He could have made an effort.

He shakes his head. "That's the thing, Em. I don't want to try. Not with these people."

I don't want to fight with him—why bother, when he'll never understand where I'm coming from? He's determined to be sullen and moody, to act the part of Emo Teen. He's not going to give Ben or anyone else a chance. Which, ironically enough, makes *him* the condescending snob.

Ben comes into the kitchen, twirling his car keys. "My Jeep is blocked in."

"It's okay," I say. "Alistair came back for me."

"Oh, great." Ben smiles at him. "Thanks, buddy."

Alistair ignores him. "Are you ready to go?" he says to me.

I nod.

Someone calls Ben's name from the other room. He leans over and gives me a quick kiss, then leaves to join his friends.

Alistair and I don't talk much on the ride back to my house, but the silence between us says everything.

✳ CHAPTER ✳
2

Alistair is sitting at our regular table at Bonus Round when I arrive the next morning, which isn't a surprise. He usually gets here first because he likes to set up the game. Settlers of Catan is our thing. The honeycomb board is spread out; the playing cards are shuffled and neatly stacked to the side, along with three mismatched mugs.

The shop smells like coffee. The *Harry Potter* soundtrack is on in the background, just below the sounds of dice hitting game boards and the grinding of the espresso machine. Alistair doesn't look up as I approach the table, a clear sign that he's still upset with me about last night. He doesn't get mad often, and while I don't want to discount his feelings, I don't really understand them. This whole situation is weird, but maybe it's just us adjusting to me really liking someone—especially when that someone is a person he hates.

"Marisol's on her way," Alistair says as I unwind my cable-knit scarf and shrug out of my jacket.

"Great." I plunk down in the worn leather club chair across from him, in front of the blue game pieces. I pick up the mocha with extra whipped cream he ordered for me. I need this coffee. Ben ended up texting me very late last night, after all his friends left. I smile, heat blooming in my chest. This is all so crazy and exciting and I still can't quite believe it's happening. That *he's* happening, to me.

I wish I could talk to Alistair about this. It should be easy because he's my friend, but it's not. There's a wall between us, and I have no idea how to scale it; I just know that something shifted between us last night, and now it's next-level awkward.

I take a sip of my lukewarm mocha, trying to think of something to say to break the tension. While Alistair fiddles with his tiny white houses, probably strategizing how he's going to win this game—which is pointless, because, hello, I am the master of Catan—I glance around, wishing Marisol would hurry up and get here and help defuse the tension. In the corner, a group of college kids is playing Dungeons and Dragons. A row of old-school video game machines are pushed against the back wall—Pac-Man, Frogger, Space Invaders—just waiting for someone to slip a quarter into them. Someone has spelled out several pretty colorful swear words with the Velcro tiles on the huge Scrabble board mounted to the brick wall. This happens a lot, but the staff are usually quick to catch it.

"Sorry, sorry," Marisol says, bursting through the door. Her cheeks are flushed from the cold, but beneath that, her face is pale. Dark rings circle her eyes. Her hair is pulled into a tangled ponytail.

"You're not feeling any better?" I ask. It occurs to me that I was so caught up in Ben last night that I never asked Alistair what was wrong with her. I'm a terrible friend.

Marisol shakes her head and the movement makes her wince. "I should have listened to my own advice and not touched that vodka punch." She rubs her forehead. "That stuff was pure evil."

Alistair wordlessly slides her mug across the table to her. She sits down beside me and says, "And how was your night?" to me in a singsong voice.

I steal a quick glance at Alistair. His eyes meet mine and then dart away, like he can't bear to look at me.

"Um, it was good." I don't want to talk about Ben in front of him, and I'm pretty sure that he doesn't want to hear about him.

Marisol raises her eyebrows. "Just good? You disappeared with Ben Griffin for hours, and all you have to say is that it was good?"

I can't help smiling. "We weren't gone for hours."

"You were gone long enough," she replies.

Before Marisol can ask me anything else, Alistair picks up the dice to determine who goes first. He rolls an eleven, then Marisol follows with an eight. I frown when the dice add up to three for me, because it means I'll be going last, which isn't ideal.

Alistair starts placing his white road and settlement pieces on the game board, setting the pieces down a little harder than necessary.

Marisol shoots me a questioning look. *What's up with him?*

I shrug. I probably should have warned her that we aren't really speaking. Honestly, I don't get why he's so mad at me. I know that he doesn't like Ben, but his reaction is kind of over-the-top. I mean, I'm not mad that he kissed Camila.

Okay, maybe I'm a little bit mad—but that's only because Camila is the worst and he can do much better. And maybe I'm a tiny bit jealous. Obviously, there's something between Alistair and me, some under-the-surface feelings that neither of us is willing to admit to. Which is really for the best, because acting on those feelings would just mess with everything. He must know that.

Marisol and I set up our roads and settlements. Alistair deals out the resource cards and we start the game.

From the beginning, it's clear that Alistair is in it to win it. After fifteen minutes, his white game pieces are already dominating the board. I need to play smarter or I'm going to lose, and that just can't happen. I've won the past six games, and there's no way I'm giving up my crown. Not without a fight, anyway.

Marisol keeps sneaking looks back and forth between Alistair and me. We play in relative silence—very unlike us. I study my resource cards. I need one more ore card to build a city, which will gain me an extra point. Marisol has no cards left—she played them all on her last hand—so I'll have to trade with Alistair.

"I'll give you a grain card for an ore," I say.

He shakes his head. "Nope."

"Nope you don't have one, or nope you're not going to trade with me?"

"Nope I'm not going to trade with you."

I roll my eyes. Seriously?

Ten minutes later, Marisol is dragging behind, but Alistair is still a point ahead of me—and dangerously close to winning the game—when I secure the largest army card, which pushes me right over the ten-point finish line.

"Ha!" I say, raising my arms in victory. Alistair snorts and shakes his head. He's never been a sore loser. Then again, I don't usually lord my wins over him like that. All right, maybe I do, but I probably shouldn't have done it today, given his mood.

"What is going on with you guys?" Marisol says as Alistair sweeps his game pieces off the board and separates his white roads and settlements into little piles. I don't know what to tell her, and I guess neither does he, so we don't say anything.

But before we can get the game set up again, Ben texts. He's with Olivia and her boyfriend, Drew, at the outdoor ice rink, and he wants to know if I'll meet up with them.

I bite my lip. Sundays are sacred. Alistair, Marisol, and I always spend them at Bonus Round. But it's a lot less fun when Alistair is broody and the truth is, I really want to see Ben.

"I have to go," I say, standing up.

"What? Why?" Marisol says.

I put on my jacket. "I forgot I told Ben I'd meet up with him. Sorry." But I know I don't sound that sorry at all.

For the first time all morning, Alistair looks at me, but I avoid his eyes.

"So that's it?" he says. "He just snaps his fingers and you run?"

"It's not like that."

But it kind of is. And I wish that he'd understand and cut me some slack.

Instead, Alistair leans back in his chair and crosses his arms. "You're ditching us for that—"

"Al," Marisol says. "Don't."

"I'm not ditching you," I say. But we all know that I am. And I feel bad about it, but not bad enough not to go.

I grab my scarf. "I'll talk to you guys later."

Alistair calls my name, but I'm already out the door. And I don't look back.

CHAPTER 3

Today was perfect. Ice skating, hot chocolate, holding Ben's hand as I wobbled like a baby deer around the outdoor rink. And then, after blueberry pancakes at the diner with Olivia and Drew, Ben's room, where we spent most of the afternoon getting to know each other better.

Now, hours later, I'm lying in my own bed, smiling into the darkness. My phone buzzes. I reach over and grab it off my nightstand, expecting another message from Ben, but instead it's Alistair.

Can you come outside for a minute?

I frown and sit up, pull back my curtain. It's almost midnight and it's below freezing and snowing pretty heavily, but there's Alistair, standing underneath the streetlamp across from my house. Staring up at my window.

He gives me a small wave.

What is he doing here?

I climb out of bed and quietly slip past my parents' room and down the stairs. I pull my puffy jacket on over my pajamas and step into my winter boots.

The street is quiet. Most of the lights in the neighboring houses are off, everybody already tucked into bed. It's so cold that I can see my breath. My boots leave deep impressions in the snow as I walk toward Alistair. He's still waiting under the streetlight in a jean jacket that's not nearly warm enough for this weather and those pointless fingerless gloves. Snowflakes have gathered in his dark hair, like stars in the night sky.

I've almost reached him when I slip on a patch of ice. Alistair grabs my arm, but instead of steadying me, he loses his balance too, and we fall in a tangled heap to the ground.

He groan-laughs, rubbing his hip. "I can't believe you took me down with you," he says. "You all right?"

I'm lying on my back, the streetlight shining in my eyes. My butt aches from landing on the hard-packed snow, but otherwise I'm okay. "I'm fine."

Alistair gets to his feet and holds out his hand to help me up. But once I'm standing, he doesn't let go of my hand. He doesn't move away. He just stands there, barely a breath away, his eyes dropping to my lips.

My heart flutters. He's never looked at me like this before. Like he's thinking about kissing me.

Or maybe he has. Maybe he's looked at me this way before and I just haven't looked back at him.

I'm light-headed at the thought of closing the last bit of

distance between us and doing something that we could never undo.

What am I doing? This is Alistair. Hooking up with him would be a mistake. What would happen to our friendship if things didn't work out between us?

I let go of his hand. "Why are you here?" The words come out a bit more abruptly, more accusatory, then I intended them to. It makes me wonder what I'm really annoyed about—that Alistair's shown up in the middle of the night, or that I'm having these unwelcome feelings for him. And even if I could put my worry about ruining our friendship aside, it doesn't even matter, because he's too late—I'm with Ben now. He may not officially be my boyfriend yet, but we're definitely heading in that direction.

Alistair doesn't say anything for a long moment. It's so quiet that I can hear the snow falling.

He clears his throat. "I wanted to know if you want to go to winter formal," he says. "With me."

I gape at him. A school dance is the last place that Alistair would ever voluntarily be seen, but he's asking me to go with him anyway. As his date. It's so un-Alistair-like that I'm momentarily thrown.

My throat feels thick as I tuck my hands inside my jacket pockets. "Ben already asked me."

Alistair winces. He glances away from me. "So, what? He's your boyfriend now?"

I shrug. I have nothing to feel bad about. I should be happy—I *was* happy, until he showed up outside my window—

but instead I feel hollow. I'm shaking, but I don't think it has anything to do with the cold.

He gives me one of his lopsided smiles and my heart aches. This is the worst. "Okay, well. No big deal," he says. "Just thought I'd ask. Uh, I should probably get going. Before we both freeze to death."

I nod. "Okay. Talk to you tomorrow?"

"Yeah, sounds good."

My chest tightens as I head back toward my house. I just want to get inside and crawl back into my bed, and hopefully the next time I see Alistair, we can pretend this conversation never happened. We can go back to ignoring these feelings we have for each other, and just stay friends.

I'm almost at my door when I hear him hurrying to catch up with me, his high-top Converse crunching through the snow.

"Actually, Em," he says as I turn back around. "There's something I need to tell you." He's standing at the bottom of the stairs, looking up at me, his eyes bright. "And I need to do it now before I completely lose my nerve. So just listen, okay?"

I'm not sure that I want to know what he's about to say. In fact, I'm pretty sure that I *don't* want to know—he's going to ruin everything—but he's already walking up the steps. He stops in front of me.

"If you're a bird, I'm a bird," he says.

I blink. Huh?

"I could be fun, if you want," Alistair continues. The tips of his ears are red. "Pensive . . . smart . . . superstitious, brave. I can be light on my feet. I could be whatever you want. You just tell me what you want and I'll be that for you."

Wait. Is he quoting from *The Notebook*?

My stomach flips. I think he is. Marisol and I have made him watch that movie a million times. He always pretends to hate it.

Alistair sighs and rubs the back of his neck. "Look, what I'm trying to say is that I—"

"I know what you're trying to say," I interrupt. I just can't believe he's saying it. I can't believe that he's doing this now. The depth of feeling in his eyes scares me and I don't know how to handle it. I'm not ready for this. I'm not ready for him. He reaches for my arm but I step away.

We've been friends forever. I don't want to mess with what we have. Besides, I can't just turn off my feelings for Ben. And, more important, I don't want to.

Alistair exhales and tips his head back to look at the sky. The silence between us stretches into awkwardness. "I don't get it," he says finally. "Why him?"

I shake my head. I don't know what to say. The truth is kind of embarrassing to admit, and it won't make anything between us easier: Ben is good-looking, the most popular guy in school, and he likes me. Out of all the girls in our school, he noticed *me*. Is it so wrong to want to be popular, to spend weekends doing something other than playing board games? To want a different life from the one I have?

But Alistair wouldn't understand—being popular isn't something he aspires to—so I just say, "Why *not* him?"

He scowls. "I can think of a few million reasons."

"Come on. You don't even know him."

"And I don't want to," he says. "Em, seriously, he's a jerk. How do you not see that?"

"People can change."

He shakes his head sadly. "Yeah, I guess they can." Then he turns and walks away, leaving me alone on the porch, my eyes burning with tears as I watch him disappear down the street.

SIX MONTHS LATER

✴ CHAPTER ✴
4

"Buongiorno. Cosa vorresti per cena?" Mom says when I walk into the kitchen. She's sitting on a stool at the island, her laptop open to an online language program. She's been on the fast track to learn Italian ever since she booked our trip to Italy last month.

"Translation, please," I say as Napoleon, our German shepherd, nudges his wet nose against my bare leg.

"What would you like for dinner?"

I scratch him behind his ear. "Sounds better in Italian."

"Pretty much everything does," Mom agrees. She tucks a strand of her silver hair behind her ear. I hate that she stopped dyeing it—it makes her look old.

"Actually, I'm not staying for dinner," I say. "I'm going out with Ben."

My mom's lips tighten almost imperceptibly. She's getting better at keeping her thoughts about my boyfriend to herself, but I know that doesn't mean her opinion of him has changed. Still, we don't fight about him quite as much as we used to.

I open the fridge and grab a pitcher of iced tea. "Dad in bed?"

She nods, her lips now pressed together so hard that they've almost completely disappeared.

My dad has been sleeping a lot lately. He's been depressed for months, ever since his company went through a merger and he was let go from his position as sales director. It hasn't helped that he's had trouble finding work. You'd think the more experience someone has the better, but it turns out that's not the case. He's overqualified for most of the jobs he's applied for. And not many companies are looking to hire someone who's only a handful of years away from retirement.

My mom thought a vacation might help, even though we can't afford one. She's always dreamed of going to the Amalfi Coast. I've spent hours online looking at photos of pastel houses perched on jagged cliffs, imagining myself swimming in the vast blue stretch of the Mediterranean or walking along the cobblestone streets, taking in the quaint shops. But instead of seeing it as a relaxing distraction, some family time, and a much-needed chance to recharge, my dad is getting really stressed out by the cost of the trip. As a result, the level of tension in our household is at an all-time high.

"*Che cosa mi consiglia?*" the computerized woman says.

"*Che cosa mi consiglia?*" Mom repeats.

There are no clean glasses for my iced tea, so I grab one from the dishwasher to rinse out. I turn on the faucet and water sprays everywhere. I quickly shut the water off, but not before my T-shirt is totally soaked.

Mom sighs. "I guess we can add that to the list of things that don't work in this house."

I know she's referring to the closet door that has slipped off its track and the ceiling fan that no longer spins, not my dad, but in the case of the worst timing ever, he walks in. And I can tell from the way his face falls that he thinks it's a knock against him.

Mom obviously catches her blunder too, because she blushes. "I'll call the plumber."

"No need," Dad replies. He's wearing an old, holey Rolling Stones T-shirt, sweatpants, and three days' worth of scruff on his cheeks. His dandelion puff of rust-red hair badly needs a comb. His hair color is the only physical attribute we share. Everything else about me is my mom. "I can fix it."

Mom and I exchange a skeptical glance. My dad is not exactly handy. In fact, I can't remember a time when he's ever done more than change a light bulb.

This probably isn't going to end well.

"Are you sure, Jeff?" Mom says. "Wouldn't it be easier just to—"

"I can fix it," he repeats, an edge of irritation in his voice. "I just need a wrench." He pauses. "Do we have a wrench?"

Mom shrugs.

While Dad disappears to search for the tools, I pop into my room to change into dry clothes. I grab a T-shirt from my closet, trying to avoid looking at the joker cards that paper one of my walls. Alistair and I started collecting them back in elementary school. I can't even recall why. It was strange, but we used to find them everywhere. He claimed it was magic.

My throat thickens. I should probably take the cards down. I don't know why I haven't already. Maybe because they remind me of him and how we used to be, before I torpedoed our friendship.

* * *

"Em, you can't keep canceling on us," Marisol said, cornering me at my locker a few weeks after I chose Ben over Alistair. I'd barely spent any time with my friends since then, I'd been so swept up in Ben and my exciting new life.

The bell rang. "I know, I know," I said. "I'm *that girl*, the one who's always with her boyfriend. I know we hate that girl. I'm sorry. It's just that—"

"Em," Ben called down the hallway. I glanced over at him. He twirled his car keys, his signal that he was anxious to leave for the day. I quickly shoved my biology textbook into my bag and bent down to root around in the bottom of my locker for my calculus homework.

Marisol squeezed my arm. "We just miss you."

"I miss you guys too," I said.

And I did miss them. But the truth of it was, I'd been steering clear of Alistair. I told myself it was to spare his feelings, but deep down, I knew it was because I didn't want to deal with the complicated emotions that washed over me every time I saw him.

"Em, come on," Ben said.

My shoulders tightened. I slammed my locker door shut and turned to smile at Marisol. "I have to go. I'll text you later and we'll catch up. I promise!"

But somehow I never got around to sending her that message. Days turned into weeks, weeks into months, and soon enough my eyes would skip over Alistair and Marisol when I saw them in the cafeteria. The three of us had once been entwined like the roots of a tree, but now we'd become strangers. All because of me.

* * *

If they only knew how much I wish that I could take it all back. I'd do everything differently, if I only had the chance.

Ben honks to let me know that he's outside. I grab my hoodie and run down the stairs and out the door. I know how much he hates to be kept waiting.

* * *

Ben and I trail behind Olivia and Drew as they wander from booth to booth at the summer night market, trying to decide what to eat next. Drew has already worked his way through a bowl of fried pickles, two corn dogs, and a blooming onion, and we've only been here for half an hour.

He turns around and points to a glass case lined with a rainbow of different candies and fat slices of fudge. "Bacon-wrapped caramel apple?"

Ben shakes his head. "I'll pass."

"We'll all pass," Olivia says, lightly shoving Drew's shoulder. "How about something that has some nutritional value?"

Drew grins at her, all wolfy white teeth. "Apples have nutritional value."

"Not if they're covered in caramel," she replies.

"Bacon is protein." He pats his stomach. "And I'm a growing boy."

Olivia yanks him away and we keep walking. The air is smoky and thick with the smell of barbecue and fried food. We came early to avoid the worst of the crowds, but now that the sun has set, the lines for everything are getting longer. The night market is waking up, and the neon lights from the few rides—the Tilt-A-Whirl, the Ferris wheel—are flickering to life.

Drew stops dead in front of a red-striped booth, inside which a man is flipping hamburgers. He stares slack-jawed at the sign advertising burgers on glazed doughnuts instead of regular buns.

I wrinkle my nose. "Yuck. Who would think to put those two things together?"

"An evil genius, that's who," Drew says, taking out his wallet. "I mean, I like hamburgers and I like doughnuts. Put them together and it can only increase the deliciousness."

"You can't be serious," Olivia says as he takes out his wallet.

"As a heart attack," he replies.

She crosses her arms. "A heart attack is what you'll get if you keep eating junk."

"Who are you, the food police?" Drew walks up to the booth, leaving her staring after him.

Olivia huffs out a breath, but a minute later she joins him at the window.

"You want something?" Ben asks me, in that slightly bored tone I've noticed creeping into his voice more and more when we're together.

I shake my head. I had some fries when we first got here and I don't want to eat too much, in case they decide they want to go on some rides later. I've made that mistake before and it didn't end well.

A family is clearing off a picnic table nearby. Ben and I pounce, before anyone else can grab it. We sit on opposite sides of the table and he drums his fingers against the wooden top.

"I can't believe you're going to be gone for an entire month," he says, his eyes following a girl in a blue sundress as she walks by.

I clench my teeth. I've asked him at least a thousand times not to ogle other girls in front of me—super disrespectful—but it's like his eyes are magnets, drawn to every female in the vicinity.

I cross my arms. I can't wait to get out of here. Mostly because I'm excited to be going to Italy, but also because I need some time away from Ben. Being his girlfriend has chipped away at me. As it turns out, Alistair was right—Ben hasn't really upgraded from his middle-school self. The bully that I was so sure he'd left behind is still there, under the surface.

I've thought a lot about breaking up with him. The problem is, the second I dump Ben, I know I'll be banished back to the fringes. After the way I treated Alistair and Marisol, I don't expect them to welcome me back with open arms. I'll spend my senior year lonely and friendless. And while that may be no less than I deserve, I'm not quite brave enough to try. Crappy friends are better than no friends.

Drew carries two paper plates over to the table, Olivia following behind him holding a blue drink served in a giant light bulb. He sets one of the doughnut-hamburgers in front of Ben.

"It's called a Luther burger," he says, plunking down beside Ben. "Named after the old-timey soul singer who invented it."

"Well, thank you, Luther." Ben picks up his burger and takes a bite. His eyes drift shut and he makes a happy grunting noise as he chews.

I hate that happy grunting chewing noise.

Olivia sits down beside me. "You'll never believe who was behind us in line," she says, smiling coyly across the table at Ben.

"Who?"

"Amy."

Ben starts to choke on his burger. He coughs, his face red. Drew thumps him on the back.

Olivia's smile widens. "So, you do remember her. She wasn't sure you would. You were pretty drunk that night."

"Who's Amy?" I ask.

"Just some girl," Ben replies, avoiding my eyes.

"Some girl that Ben hooked up with and then totally ghosted," Olivia says, shaking her head. "Oh, but don't worry, Em. She was B.E."

B.E. stands for "before Emelia." Shorthand for anything—or anyone—that happened before Ben and I got together.

And as it turns out, there's a lot that happened before we got together.

I know Ben has been with other people, but I'm not into hearing all the gory details. Unfortunately for me, Olivia is all about the gory details.

Ben slumps down in his seat, but there's really nowhere to hide. "Did she see me?"

"Uh, yeah," Drew says. "But I wouldn't worry about her coming over here. She didn't seem too anxious to reconnect."

Olivia fiddles with the straw in her light bulb drink. "You should have at least texted the poor girl back."

"Yeah, well. Lesson learned." Ben frowns and sets his hamburger down. He wipes his sticky, glaze-covered fingers on a napkin.

I'm not surprised that he ghosted her. Ben doesn't like to talk feelings, and he doesn't deal well with confrontation—character traits that we have in common. I know that what he did was inexcusable, but I can't help feeling some sympathy for him. After all, I basically did the same thing with Alistair and Marisol.

So maybe we deserve each other.

✳ CHAPTER ✳
5

After Drew finishes his burger, he decides he wants a deep-fried Mars bar. Olivia rolls her eyes, but she doesn't say anything. We hold the table while Drew and Ben wander off to find the booth.

Olivia immediately pulls out her phone and starts scrolling through Instagram, dutifully ignoring me. Our boyfriends are best friends, so we're thrown together a lot, and we make the best of it. Or I try to, anyway. Olivia mostly ignores me, especially if we're left alone together.

I think about what a great friend Marisol was and I feel sick. I can't believe I traded her in for Olivia Brandt.

I sigh as I watch people passing by. When there's a break in the crowd, I notice a playing card on the ground, over by the recycling bin. Without thinking, I slide off the bench and bend down to pick it up. I flip the card over, revealing a black-and-white fool's cap set on top of a grinning skull. The joker.

I can't believe it. I haven't found a joker in ages. Although maybe the reason I haven't found one lately is because I stopped looking for them.

"Ew," Olivia says, wrinkling her nose. "Why are you picking up garbage?"

"It's not garbage." I tuck the card into the back pocket of my shorts. I should just throw it out, but I know that I won't. It's a throwback to my old life and it means something to me. I don't trust her to understand.

"It's all bent and dirty and it was left on the ground." Olivia's looking at me like I've morphed into a wild animal or something. "That's the very definition of garbage."

I laugh, hoping she doesn't think that I'm totally weird, but that train left the station a long time ago. She shakes her head and turns back to her phone.

I'm so tired of having to act cool just to fit in. I can't wait to be on the plane to Italy, where I won't have to worry about saying or doing the wrong thing for an entire month. Of course, once my vacation ends, I'll end up where I started—back here with Ben and his terrible friends.

Maybe I'll just stay in Italy forever.

Ben and Drew finally return. Drew pushes up the brim of his trucker hat and says, "There's no line at the Scrambler," through a mouthful of Mars bar. "Let's go."

"Seriously? You just ate," Olivia says. "You're going to puke."

"I'm willing to take that risk." He grabs her hand and pulls her off the bench.

Ben holds his hand out to me. My stomach lurches at the thought of the Spider's metal octopus arms spinning the seats through the air, but I weave my fingers through his and we follow after Drew and Olivia. As we're walking through the night market, I spot Alistair and Marisol coming toward us.

There they are. My ghosts of friendships past. Like I've somehow conjured them out of thin air, just by thinking of them.

And God, Alistair looks good. My cheeks flush. How did I never notice that before? His dark curls fall in a messy tangle, just begging to be pushed off his forehead. He's wearing jeans and the VOTE FOR PEDRO T-shirt I bought him for his birthday last year. I wonder what it means that he's wearing it tonight—does he still think of me, or has it become just another T-shirt in his closet?

He laughs at something Marisol says and the sound carries over the crowd, piercing right through me.

I miss that laugh.

I miss my friends.

Running into them when I'm with Ben is not ideal—I can't trust Ben to be the best version of himself, especially when he's around Drew—so I tug on his hand before he notices Alistair and Marisol.

"I know a shortcut," I say, praying that they'll listen to me for once. But it's too late—I can tell by the way Drew's back stiffens that he's already seen Alistair. Sure enough, he looks over his shoulder at Ben and me, an evil smile on his face. "Nerd alert," he says.

My adrenaline spikes as Drew turns back around. He quickens his step until he's almost in front of Alistair and Marisol.

Alistair's eyes meet mine a split second before Drew shoulder-checks him, knocking him off balance and sending him stumbling into Marisol.

"Watch it, dude," Drew says.

Marisol scowls at him. "You're the one who pushed him. Why don't you watch it," she says. I can feel Olivia silently judging her off-brand jean overalls and scuffed Doc Marten boots with the neon laces, her wild curls pulled back with a dollar-store headband.

"You always let your girlfriend fight your battles for you?" Drew asks.

Alistair sighs. "The first rule of Fight Club is you do not talk about Fight Club."

Drew blinks. He reaches out and pokes Alistair hard in the chest. "You asking for a fight, son?"

Alistair holds up his hands. "I'm definitely not looking for a fight. It was just a joke. Dad."

"You think you're funny?" Drew takes another step toward him until they're almost touching. Alistair is taller, but Drew is stockier, a wall of muscle—and used to fighting.

Alistair smirks. "Sometimes," he replies as Marisol tugs on his arm, trying to draw him away.

My eyes widen. What is he doing? Is he trying to antagonize Drew? Not a good idea.

Drew's upper lip curls and he puffs out his chest. "Well, I don't think you're funny. At all."

"Do something," I say to Ben.

"What do you want me to do?" he replies.

I glare at him.

Ben rolls his eyes. "Stop worrying. Drew's just playing with him. He's not actually going to do anythi—"

Drew pulls his arm back and sucker punches Alistair in the stomach. I watch in horror as Alistair grunts and doubles over, gasping for air. Marisol squeals and rests her hand on his back. Several people walking past glance over at us, but no one stops. Before I can even ask Alistair if he's okay, Ben drags me into the crowd, after Drew and Olivia.

I'm shaking as he pulls me in the direction of the Scrambler. I can't believe that just happened. Why did I just stand there? How could I let Drew treat them like that?

Shame burns through me. My throat is thick as we join the line for the ride. Ben, Drew, and Olivia have already moved on from the altercation, like punching someone in the stomach for no reason is acceptable behavior.

I wish I could say I'm surprised, but this is just the latest example of how they're the worst. It wasn't too long after Ben and I started dating that I realized he hadn't really changed, but I still managed to convince myself that the good outweighed the bad.

And I'm not any better than them. If I was, I would have spoken up one of the hundreds of times that I've seen them treat people badly.

I should have said something tonight.

Maybe it's not too late.

I bite my lip. Alistair's wearing the T-shirt I gave him. He probably wouldn't still have it, much less wear it, if he hated me. What if there's still a chance to fix things with him and Marisol?

I could tell them that I'm sorry and I've made a terrible mistake. I'll tell Alistair that I wish I'd chosen him instead. Maybe he'll forgive me. Maybe he'll give me another chance.

My pulse starts to race. Ben is busy talking to Drew and Olivia, so he doesn't notice when I drop his hand and start to weave my way through the line of people behind us.

"Em, where are you going?" Ben calls after me.

I hurry through the night market. Alistair and Marisol have moved on—they're no longer where we left them. I'm sweating, hoping that they haven't gone home, when I see Alistair sitting on top of a picnic table all by himself.

"Are you okay?"

He eyes me warily. "I've been better."

I glance around for Marisol.

"She went to get me a drink," he says.

I swallow. This is my moment—my chance to apologize and tell him how I really feel. But the words stick in my throat. I don't even know where to start. And from the way he's scowling at me, I'm not at all sure that he's interested in hearing anything I have to say.

And I can't blame him.

A hand shoots past me, holding a bottle of Gatorade. "They only had the red kind," Marisol says.

"Thanks." Alistair twists off the cap and takes a long drink while I gather the nerve to look over at Marisol. I'm surprised to see that she's not alone—she's with Jiya Malik.

Marisol's staring at me, her eyes narrowed. "Why are you here?"

"I . . . came to see if Alistair was all right."

She snorts. "All of a sudden you care how he's doing?"

"Mari," Alistair says.

Before I can respond and tell her that I never stopped caring, Jiya slides on top of the picnic table beside Alistair. He gives her a small, private smile and reaches for her hand, and that's when it hits me, full force.

I've been replaced.

There's no going back.

Alistair has moved on.

I blink back the tears that are suddenly stinging my eyes.

"Okay, well," I say, hoping they can't hear the tremble in my voice. "Looks like you're taken care of, so . . . maybe I'll see you around."

Ben's my ride, but I'm not ready to face him yet, so I wander aimlessly through the night market, feeling miserable. Soon I find myself near the chain-link fence that marks the end of the market. A deep purple tent that I've never noticed before is tucked away in the corner. A sign is pinned to the front of the tent: YOUR FATE IS IN YOUR HANDS, written in cursive above a black-and-white illustration of an open hand.

I feel a magnetic pull toward the tent. The curtains are pulled back, revealing a fold-up table laid out with stacks of tarot cards, tall candles with pictures of saints, and a clay bowl filled with a variety of colorful rocks. There's a diffuser in the corner, and the scent of patchouli cuts through the popcorn-and-fried-food smell of the night market.

The woman working in the booth smiles at me. She looks

exactly like the type of strange, witchy person you'd expect to see selling stuff like this: long, wavy white hair, a row of colorful bangles on her arm, a flowy patchwork skirt. An orange butterfly barrette is clipped above her left ear, like it's making a nest in her hair.

"You want a reading, darling?" she asks. "Twenty-five bucks for twenty minutes."

I shake my head. I only brought twenty dollars. I can't spare the time, even if I did have enough money—I have to find Ben before he strands me here.

"Just looking," I say. I sift through the bowl of rocks. My eye catches on a stone that looks slightly different from the rest. It's a translucent yellow with thin gold threads shooting through it, about the size of a walnut. I pick it up. The rock is strangely warm in my hand.

The woman gestures at the stone. "Rutilated quartz. A very powerful crystal," she says. "Is there something that you regret in the past? Something that you wish to change?"

A shiver goes through me. How did she know that?

Probably just a good guess. She must be trained to read body language or something.

"Doesn't everyone have something in their past that they'd like to change?" I reply.

"Some more than others." She smiles. "That crystal can help you."

I stare at her. Wait. Is she suggesting that this stone can change the past? That I could use it to fix things with Alistair and Marisol? Because I don't believe that anything—least of all a rock—could change Alistair's mind about me. Our friendship is way beyond repair.

But, then again . . . what if it did help? I glance down at the rock. There's something hypnotizing about the web of gold threads running through it. And I like the way it feels in my hand. Maybe I shouldn't be so quick to dismiss the idea . . . I mean, it is kind of weird, the way I found that joker and then stumbled across this tent.

"I should warn you—you want to be very careful with that crystal," the woman adds. "Change one thing from the past and you change everything about your future."

My face heats up. This is ridiculous. I can't believe I'm standing here, actually considering buying a rock in the vain hope that it might work some kind of magic and make Alistair and Marisol forgive me.

But . . . I would do anything to go back and choose Alistair. And while it seems highly unlikely that a rock could actually make that happen, my heart really wants to believe that it's possible.

"So how does this work, exactly?" I ask.

She leans her elbows on the table. "Put it under your pillow tonight. Before you fall asleep, focus on the thing in your past that you most want to change. In the morning, when you wake up, that particular problem will have resolved itself."

I lift an eyebrow. "That's it?" I don't know what I was expecting, but it seems way too easy. Shouldn't there be a chant or a ritual sacrifice or something?

"Well, you have to really concentrate," she says. "And you

need to be very careful about what you wish for. So, make sure it's something that you really, truly want to change. If you pull one thread in a sweater, then the whole thing can unravel, you see?"

I have to admit, the idea of my sweater unraveling or whatever makes me a bit uneasy. What if, by choosing Alistair instead of Ben, I send my life in a completely unexpected direction?

It doesn't matter. Whatever my new future holds, having my friends back will be worth it.

"I'll take it," I say, pulling out my wallet. I check over my shoulder to make sure Ben isn't behind me. If he catches me in this booth, buying a rock, then I'll never hear the end of it. He doesn't believe in magic or palm readers or anything else that this woman is selling.

I feel a little foolish as she takes the money from my outstretched hand. The crystal costs fifteen dollars, which seems suspiciously cheap for something that she swears is going to change my life.

"Now, I should mention, this crystal won't bring anyone back from the dead or anything like that," she says, dropping it into a little blue velvet bag and pulling the strings shut. "So if that's what you're looking to fix . . ."

I shake my head. The only thing that I'll be raising from the dead is my relationship with my friends—and, hopefully, Alistair's feelings for me. If this even works. But after what happened tonight, I feel like it's the only chance I have to make things right again.

"One more thing," the woman says, handing me the pouch.

"This crystal can only be used once. There's no going back if you don't like the results. And no returns."

The look on her face is kind of ominous. But then her expression clears and her face breaks into a smile.

"Good luck," she says.

"Don't forget to pack your inhaler," my mom says later that night.

I roll my eyes. This is the third time she's reminded me. We don't leave for Italy until tomorrow afternoon, but she's buzzing around the house as if we're already late for our flight.

She hands me a list of things I still need to pack, instead of trusting that I know I need to bring underwear and good walking shoes. *Inhaler* is underlined twice.

"And remember, no cell phone," she says. My mom is insisting that we be "in the moment" on this vacation, which means that we need to leave our phones at home.

I sigh. "Mom. I *know.*"

"Come and say goodbye to Napoleon."

"You're taking him now?" It's almost eleven thirty. "Why can't we keep him until tomorrow?"

Napoleon's going to be staying with my mom's friend Maya

while we're away. She has a farm, with lots of space for him to run. She's promised to play Frisbee with him every day, but still, I feel bad about leaving him for an entire month.

"I have too much to do tomorrow," she says. "I was planning to take him earlier this evening, but you left the house so fast. I knew you'd want a chance to say goodbye to him. Lucky for you, Maya is a night owl."

I follow her downstairs. My parents' suitcases are already in the hall, lined up like soldiers standing at attention. Napoleon is waiting by the front door, wagging his tail, totally oblivious that my mom is about to take him away.

I kneel down and bury my face in his neck. My mom gives me a minute before clipping on his leash. Napoleon starts to dance around, thinking he's going for a late-night walk.

"Let's go, buddy," she says. She picks up the bag she packed for him, containing his toys and treats. I watch from the window as she loads him into the car.

A string of loud swear words comes from the direction of the kitchen. I wander in to find my dad's legs sticking out from underneath the sink, a variety of tools splayed out on the tile around him. He slides out and sits up, his face flushed. He wipes the back of his hand across his brow.

"Fixing a leak is a lot harder than it looks," he says, sighing. "Don't tell your mother, but if I was to do this over again, I wouldn't have tried to fix it myself. I'd have called a plumber."

If he could do it over again . . .

My stomach flutters. His words remind me of the crystal I bought at the night market tonight. What if it really is a magical, time-turning rock? What if it really can change my past and make things right with Alistair and Marisol?

It seems totally impossible, but I have nothing to lose by trying it. So, after I finish packing everything on the list my mom gave me, I dig the crystal out from my bag and place it under my pillow, just like the palm reader instructed me to.

Then I get into bed and close my eyes, replaying that winter night Alistair showed up at my house. I think about the intense look in his eyes when he told me how he felt about me.

If you're a bird, I'm a bird, he said. *I could be fun if you want. I could be—*

Instead of letting Alistair finish, I rewrite the memory and do what I should have done that night—I throw my arms around him and kiss him. I smile in the darkness. And, for the first time in a long time, I relax. Maybe everything will work out after all.

* * *

I wake up early the next morning to the sound of someone banging around downstairs. The sun is filtering through my blinds, casting stripes of light on my carpet. I groan, about to roll over and go back to sleep, when I notice something is very different about my room.

I sit up, suddenly totally awake. When I went to bed, my walls were the same apple green they'd been since I was in sixth grade. Now they're a shocking purple, a color so deep and bright that it makes my eyes water.

All the air is sucked out of my lungs as I glance around my room, taking in all the unfamiliar details—a yellow hoodie that I've never seen before hanging off the back of my desk chair, a vintage travel poster for Cuba on the wall above my bed, a string of red chili-pepper lights mounted around the window.

Unless someone is playing a very elaborate prank on me, I think the crystal worked.

It actually worked.

My heart is thumping as I slide my fingers underneath my pillow. The crystal is still there, but it seems like all the heat—all the magic—has gone out of it. I stare in shock at the yellow stone in my hand. I may have bought the crystal, I may have put it under my pillow, but I didn't *really* believe that it would work.

Maybe I'm still dreaming. I mean, this can't actually be happening, right? It's just not possible.

I squeeze my eyes shut. But when I open them again, my room is still purple.

Okay, so I'm not dreaming.

I throw off my covers and slide out of bed. As soon as my feet hit the floor, I notice my fuzzy pink socks. They match the pink-striped pajamas I'm wearing. But here's the thing: When I climbed into bed last night, I was in yoga pants and an old T-shirt.

This is so super freaky.

I'm trying to calmly take everything in, but honestly, this is all blowing my mind. I walk over to the mirror on legs that feel like they're made of jelly. When I catch sight of my reflection, all my pseudo calm goes right out the window.

I let out a little scream. My hand flies up to my head. What happened to my hair? I've always kept it long, but now it's hanging in choppy layers that just barely graze my shoulders. It doesn't look bad, exactly. Just different.

Change one thing about your past and you change everything about your future.

I glance at the corner of my mirror, where I keep a photo of Ben and me. It's gone. Which makes sense, I guess, because in this reality, that photo doesn't exist.

Because Ben and I don't exist.

Because I didn't choose him. I chose Alistair instead.

I should be relieved—this is why I wanted to change my past, after all—but I can't help the waves of uneasiness washing over me. This is all so weird. The crystal hasn't scrubbed any of the memories I have of Ben and me together, or of Olivia and Drew. But none of them are going to remember that we were ever friends.

I grab my phone from my nightstand. It's still July, which means that six months have passed since I chose Ben over Alistair, but I have no memory of anything that's happened to me in this timeline. I can't remember my first kiss with Alistair or writing finals or the winter formal. I don't have a single memory.

My hands shake as I type in my password. I just need some evidence that my friendship with Alistair and Marisol is back to normal. If we're okay, then I can relax and start to piece together what's happened to me over the last half year.

I let out a breath when I see the long string of texts from

Alistair and Marisol. I don't remember any of these conversations, but they're there. This is proof that we're friends again, so no matter what my new life might look like now, this will make it all worth it.

I stand at my closed door, my hand poised on the doorknob. For better or for worse, whatever awaits me when I step out of this room is now my life.

I take a deep breath. *Stay calm. I just need to stay calm. Everything is going to be fine.* And then I open the door.

I head downstairs. When I get to the bottom, I notice our suitcases are no longer by the front door. Napoleon must hear me coming because he skids into the hall, his nails scrabbling on the hardwood floor as he rounds the corner. He bounds over to me and licks my hand.

Hmm. No suitcases and my dog is still here. Mom never took him to Maya's place yesterday, because in this reality, we're not going to Italy.

I frown. Well, that sucks. I was really looking forward to the trip. But I guess Italy will always be there, and it seems like a small price to pay to have my friends back.

"Em, is that you?" Dad calls from the kitchen.

I take a deep breath to steady myself before following Napoleon into the kitchen. Dad's at the stove, flipping pancakes. He turns around when he hears me enter and smiles at me. I'm thrown by how great he looks. Better than I've seen him look in ages. His hair is shorter, less Einsteiny, and he's freshly shaved. And he's wearing jeans instead of sweatpants.

Also, I've never seen him cook before, so that's strange. I

guess making pancakes is a skill that he's picked up in the past few months.

"Em, why aren't you dressed?" he says, exasperated. "You're going to be late."

I stare at him. Late for what?

It's summer, so it can't be school. Unless . . . oh my God, am I in summer school? Did I fail biology?

I totally failed biology.

Dad slides a blueberry pancake onto a plate and hands it to me. "If you hurry up, we can get some driving practice in before your shift starts."

I stare at him. I've been bugging my dad to teach me to drive for months—my mom is way too nervous, which, in turn, makes me nervous—but since he barely leaves the house, I don't get a lot of practice.

"Great," I say.

And not only has he been teaching me to drive, but apparently I have a job. Although I have no idea where that job might be . . . and I'm not sure how to ask Dad about it. He's going to wonder why I don't know where I work.

I take my plate over to the table.

"Where's Mom?" I ask.

Dad blinks at me. "She's in Palm Springs."

"Oh, right, ha-ha." I can feel my cheeks heating up. "I think I'm still half-asleep."

He doesn't seem convinced. "Are you feeling all right? You look flushed."

No.

Also, why is my mom in Palm Springs? When is she coming home?

All questions I can't ask him without raising his suspicions even further. There are no safe questions, really. I guess I'm just going to have to figure this stuff out for myself.

I wolf down my pancake and run back upstairs to get changed. According to the calendar in my phone, I have a shift at nine o'clock this morning. Dad was right—I'm running late. But I still don't know where it is that I'm working, so that's a problem.

How am I going to find out where I work?

Since I'm earning a paycheck, there must be a record of the deposits in my bank account. I log in, and sure enough, there are regular payments from Castle Hardware.

I smile. I work at Castle Hardware with Alistair. And I have money, for once in my life.

I find the green vest hanging in my closet. I throw it on over white shorts and a T-shirt, then quickly dart into the bathroom to brush my teeth.

I stop short. The sink is missing. There's literally just a hole where the sink used to be. The showerhead is gone, too, and a bunch of tools are piled in the bathtub. The floor is covered in a drop cloth. Basically, it's a disaster zone.

Dad comes up the stairs, Napoleon at his heels.

"What happened in here?" I ask him.

"We're renovating the bathroom." He puts his hand against my forehead. "You sure you're feeling all right? Did you hit your head or something?"

Or something.

I laugh weakly. "I just forgot."

"You forgot your mom is away and you forgot we're renovating the bathroom," he says, a note of disbelief in his voice.

I shrug.

"Emelia, pretending to have amnesia is not going to get you out of helping me finish this project," he says, crossing his arms. "I know that it hasn't exactly been smooth so far, but imagine how satisfying it will feel when we're all done."

Wait. I'm helping him renovate the bathroom?

Honestly, this might be the biggest shock of the morning so far. We know nothing about home renovation—my dad is the least handy person there is. But I guess that was before. I guess in this reality, he's Bob Vila.

"We have to get the sink in today or we'll never get all of this done before your mom gets back," he adds.

I glance at him uneasily. "Does Mom know that we're tearing up the bathroom?" I mean, I can't argue with the fact that the upgrade is necessary—everything in here was from the eighties—but my mom is super particular. I can't imagine she'll be thrilled that we've taken this on without her.

Dad stares at me, his brow furrowing. "Em, we talked about this. Your mom and I have agreed on these changes. As we told you, the real-estate agent recommended that we fix up a few rooms before we put the house on the market," he says. He puts a hand on my shoulder. "Are you sure you didn't hit your head?"

My eyes widen. Realtor? We're selling our house?

All the blood rushes from my head and I have to lean against the wall. We've lived here my entire life. My parents have never mentioned moving before.

"But where are we going to live?" I ask in a small voice.

"We haven't figured out all the details yet. But I did see an apartment downtown that I might rent," he says. "It has two bedrooms, so when you're with me, you'll have your own space."

My eyes narrow. When I'm with him? What is he talking about?

"As for your mom, I think she wants to wait until we've sold the house before she looks for something."

Before she looks for something? We're not all going to be living together?

My chest hitches as it hits me. Oh my God. My parents are getting divorced.

✳ CHAPTER ✳
7

My parents are getting divorced.

I guess this is what the palm reader meant by my sweater unraveling.

My throat closes and my eye sting with tears. I don't get it. I changed one thing in my past and I don't understand why that change made a difference in my parents' relationship. I mean, they didn't really fight that often. And, okay, I knew things hadn't been super great between them since my dad lost his job—and maybe even for a while before that—but I never thought they'd split up.

How could they do this to me?

"All set?" Dad asks me. "If we don't hustle, you're going to be late."

Right. I have to work. At the job that I just learned I have.

"I have to brush my teeth," I say.

"Okay. I'll meet you outside." Dad whistles as he walks away.

I scowl. How can he whistle when the world is ending?

I run down the stairs and into the powder room, where I find my toothbrush and makeup piled in a corner on the counter. As I'm brushing my teeth, I hear the front door open. I head outside, where Dad's waiting beside our Honda Civic.

He's still whistling.

He hands me the car keys, all nonchalant, like this is something he does all the time.

I'm suddenly all sweaty. How am I going to tell him that I don't actually know how to drive?

This is a big problem.

"I'm not feeling so great. Maybe you should drive," I say, trying to give the keys back to him.

"Don't be silly. You need the practice." He walks around to the passenger side and gets into the car.

I rub the back of my neck. I'm not sure that I'm going to be able to pull this off. It's not like I can fake driving a car. What if I get us into an accident? I should probably just confess that I don't know what I'm doing, but I don't know how to tell my dad that without tripping the alarm bells. He already suspects that something is off with me—if I tell him that I've forgotten every driving lesson he's ever given me, then he'll definitely drag me to a doctor.

You're going to be fine, I tell myself, taking a deep breath. *You can do this.*

After all, millions of people drive every day. How hard can it be?

I slip into the driver's seat and put on my seat belt. I stick the keys in the ignition and turn the car on. When I reach for the gearshift, Dad says, "Wait a minute. Aren't you forgetting something?"

Yes! Yes, Dad. I've forgotten everything!

I stare blankly at him.

"You need to adjust your mirrors," he says.

"Oh. Right."

I tip the rearview mirror down slightly like I've seen him do before, until I can clearly see out the back window, then adjust my side mirrors. I reach for the gearshift again and try to shift it from park to reverse. Except nothing happens—the gearshift doesn't budge.

"It's stuck," I say.

Dad narrows his eyes. "You need to put your foot on the brake pedal first."

"Oh. Right."

I manage to get the car started. Clutching the wheel, I press my foot against the gas pedal. But I guess I push down a little harder than I should, because the car shoots backward. I squeal and stomp on the brake and the car jerks to a stop, nearly giving us whiplash.

"Emelia," Dad says.

"Sorry, sorry."

He sighs.

This time, I back down the driveway, much slower and more smoothly. Dad gasps when I pull out into the street.

"You forgot to check over your shoulder," he scolds.

Whoops. I smile sheepishly at him.

He sighs again. "Emelia, don't look at me. Keep your eyes on the road."

"All right, all right."

God, he's just making me even more nervous. My hands are sweating and I keep having to take one of them off the wheel at a time to wipe them on my shorts. Fortunately, the streets are quiet, and aside from almost missing a stop sign, I do pretty well on the rest of the ride.

"Turn right at the next light," Dad says.

"I know where Castle Hardware is."

I pull into the almost-empty lot and park near the entrance to the squat gray stone building, grinning with relief. I did it! I got us all the way here without getting us killed!

"Well, I don't know what that was all about, but we obviously need to practice some more," Dad says. He unclenches his hands from the dashboard and unbuckles his seat belt. "We'll try again after your shift ends."

I leave the car running and climb out, wiping my sweaty hands on my shorts again. As Dad drives away, I notice Alistair's mom's minivan tucked in the corner of the lot. I know it's her van because the back window has a stick-family decal—Alistair, his mom, and his younger sister, Cameron, along with their two ancient cats, Frida and Cosmo.

My nerves kick into high gear. This is it. I'm about to see Alistair.

A huge dark green sign shaped like a medieval flag hangs above the door, CASTLE HARDWARE written on it in Gothic white letters. I walk past an outdoor display of plastic

Adirondack chairs and bags of wood chips. The glass doors slide open and I head through the turnstile, past a row of shopping carts. The store smells like soil and rubber and is blindingly white—white floors, tall white shelves, white light fixtures. It's still early, so it's pretty quiet, only a few customers pushing carts or with plastic baskets looped over their arms.

I spot Alistair standing near the paint department, talking to a woman holding a fan of blue paint chips. My heart knocks painfully against my ribs. His dark hair is a little shorter than I'm used to, but it's still long enough for me to get my fingers tangled in. The summer sun has scattered freckles across his cheeks, and his arms are tanned and more muscly than I remember. Somehow, he manages to make the ugly green Castle Hardware vest look hot.

Alistair glances over at me and our eyes meet and I swear my knees almost give out. His eyes flick back to the woman, still listening to her talk, but a small smile crosses his face, one that I know is actually meant for me.

It's been a long time since he's smiled at me. I want to run over and talk to him, but he's leading the woman down an aisle, so I guess our reunion will have to wait a few more minutes.

"You're late," a voice says from behind me.

I turn around. Violet Chen is behind the front counter. And she's glaring at me.

"Sorry," I say. "I overslept."

She snorts. "So, are you just going to stand there all day?"

I don't know Violet well. Our paths never really crossed at school—mostly because she can be kind of scary.

She raises her eyebrows, waiting for me to do something. But I'm not sure what I'm supposed to do—where do I clock in? Is there somewhere I usually stash my bag? What is my job, even? This is all stuff that I should know, considering I've worked here for the past few months. But I don't know. I don't know anything!

I have to do something, though, before Violet kills me dead with her laser-beam eyes, so I join her behind the long counter. I think it's the right move, because her shoulders relax a little. There are three cash registers, spaced a few feet apart. I shove my bag on the shelf underneath the register beside her, wondering how I'm going to get through this shift without making a complete fool of myself.

Violet has purple-streaked hair and a septum ring, and her eyes are rimmed with thick black eyeliner that looks like she drew it on with black marker. Her green vest is covered in metal buttons—a unicorn with a rainbow mane, a chocolate chip cookie wearing thick, black-framed glasses, a yellow smiley face. And a plain white one that says CUTE AS A . . .

I bite back a smile. Violet Chen, cute as a button.

"Why does your name tag say Paul?" I ask, pointing at the metal tag pinned above the buttons.

Violet reaches into the pocket of her vest and hands me a tag. "I made them for all of us."

"Okay. But why Paul?"

She blinks at me. "After my hedgehog."

The way she says this, so matter-of-factly, tells me I'm supposed to know that she has a hedgehog named Paul. I'm probably supposed to know a lot of things about her.

A customer walks up to the counter with a power drill. Violet smiles tightly at him, barely concealing her irritation at being bothered. I try to discreetly watch over her shoulder as she rings up his purchase, hoping I can figure out how to work the cash register.

She scans the drill, then silently points at the total on the screen: $68.52.

The man taps his credit card on the machine attached to the counter. A few seconds later, Violet tears off a receipt and hands it to him.

So, that doesn't look so hard.

The man leaves and the smile instantly melts off Violet's face. "I hate my life," she says, tugging on one of the silver nuts strung like pearls on a thin wire around her neck.

"Are you okay?"

"No." I think she's going to leave it at that, but a few minutes later she says, "Avery and I broke up."

I can't very well ask her who Avery is—it's clearly another thing that I'm supposed to know.

"Oh. I'm sorry," I say.

"Yeah, well." She sighs heavily and rubs her eyes, smudging her liner. "The worst part is, I didn't even see it coming. I thought we were happy. But it turns out, I was the only one who was happy—apparently she was miserable."

A bolt of guilt shoots through me. That's exactly how I felt in my relationship with Ben—miserable. Only I didn't have the guts to break up with him. I don't know what to say to make her feel better, so I don't say anything, and the silence between us soon turns awkward.

"Why are you acting weird?" she finally asks.

"I'm not." My cheeks burn.

"Yeah. You are." Her eyes narrow. "Is it because you made out with that random guy at Ryan's party? Because I've told you a million times, I'm taking that to the grave."

Huh? What party? Who's Ryan? And why would I make out with a random guy there? Alistair is my boyfriend.

Oh my God. Did I cheat on Alistair?

This is all so confusing.

Before I can ask her about this supposed make-out session, a woman starts to unload her buggy onto the counter in front of me—light bulbs, floor wax, a roll of duct tape. A baby is sitting in the front of the cart, chewing on an amber teething ring.

"Good morning," I say.

I stare at the cash register, my mind reeling. I need to sign in to unlock it, but I have no idea how to do that. And another customer has just walked up with a bag of wood chips. Violet starts to ring him through. Luckily, my customer is distracted by her baby and hasn't noticed that I haven't even started to put her order through.

I punch in my birthday—maybe I used that as my password?—and the register beeps loudly, reprimanding me for getting it wrong. I try a bunch of other number combinations, but none of them work.

This is a nightmare.

Violet gives me the side-eye. I'm about to give up and admit that I don't know what I'm doing, consequences be damned, when Alistair slips behind the counter.

"I forgot my password," I say.

"It happens."

He taps on the register, standing close enough to me that our hips brush. He smells like peppermint, and all I can think about is being alone with him. He steps back so I can scan the order. I'm slow, but I somehow manage to stumble through, even though everyone is watching me. All the customers in my line migrate over to Violet, who is a hundred times faster.

When the rush finally clears—thanks to Violet—she turns to me. "What was that about?" she asks. "It's like you've never worked a cash register before."

"I, uh, guess I'm just having an off morning."

How else can I explain it? It's not like I can tell her the truth.

Alistair touches my wrist and a thousand tiny fireworks go off through my body. "You okay, Em?"

I nod. I want to fold myself in his arms, bury my face in his neck. I want to kiss him to make up for everything, even if he doesn't know what I'm making up for. We've probably made out thousands of times over the past six months.

I reach out to straighten his name tag—his says Paul, too—and he looks at me, surprised. He smiles and there are those fireworks again, but then his face straightens, like he suddenly remembered something.

"Anyway, Avery's already seeing someone else," Violet says,

picking up our earlier conversation. "The body isn't even cold yet and she's already back out there."

"You don't know that," Alistair replies. But I notice he doesn't look at her when he says it. He doesn't look at me, either.

"I do know that. My feminine intuition is very strong." She grimaces. "Ugh. We're both on the schedule tomorrow. I'm thinking about calling in sick."

"You're going to have to face her sometime," he says. "Might as well get it over with."

Violet groans. "Why didn't I listen to you? Dating someone you work with is a terrible idea."

I wait for Alistair to correct her—after all, we're dating and we work together. But he just shrugs.

I frown. Why did he just shrug?

"Listen, why don't you come out with us later? Take your mind off everything." He slings his arm around Violet's shoulders. "We're heading to Bonus Round after work to practice for the Catan tournament."

Hold up. We're in the Catan tournament? Every year, Bonus Round holds a qualifying tournament for the big national game, usually held in a city far away from where we are. We've talked about entering before, but never seriously.

Violet makes a face. "Is that that weird board game you guys are always playing? The one with the wheat and the cows?"

"Yes, and it's not weird," he replies. "And there are no cows. Try it and I promise you'll be hooked. Right, Em?"

"Right." I'm excited that we're going to Bonus Round—and

even more excited that I'll be seeing Marisol—but I was hoping that we'd have some alone time together.

"I guess it's better then hanging out by myself in my room," Violet says.

"It's definitely better than that." He gives her a quick hug. "I'd better get back to stocking aisle three. Those boxes of floor polish aren't going to unpack themselves."

He walks away, whistling. But then he stops and turns back around, pushes his mop of dark hair out of his eyes. "Look, I know you think she was the one, but I don't," he says. "Now, I think you're just remembering the good stuff. Next time you look back, I really think you should look again."

"Huh?" Violet says.

"It's from *Five Hundred Days of Summer*." I smile. One of Alistair's favorite movies.

Violet rolls her eyes. "Of course it is," she says, but she's smiling too.

✳ CHAPTER ✳
8

"Introvert hangovers are a real thing." Marisol frowns at Alistair from across the table. "Look it up."

"I'm not doubting that they exist," he says, setting his blue road down on the game board. "I just don't think that you have one."

"I only just figured it out," she says. She ticks the list of signs off on her fingers. "I'm tired and anxious. I can't think clearly. It took me twenty minutes to decide which shade of yellow thread to use for this embroidery. I feel like I could kill someone."

Alistair gestures at the wooden hoop on her lap. She's been working on a detailed cross-stitch of a bride and groom between turns. It seems that Marisol has taken up embroidery, something she never showed an interest in before. And she's gotten so good at it over the past six months that she's opened up an Etsy shop.

"You're tired and anxious because you're taking on too many orders," he says. "You have to give yourself a break."

Marisol scowls and pushes her glasses up the bridge of her nose. "I don't have time for a break! I have to finish this before Saturday." She glances at me and her eyes narrow. "Em, why do you keep smiling at me like that?"

"Like what?" But I know I have a goofy smile on my face. Despite the news about my parents and the fact that we're selling our house—which I am trying very hard not to think about—I can't help but be happy to be here at Bonus Round with them again. The place hasn't changed: Mario and Luigi are still painted on the window, pumping their fists in the air. The Monopoly man is still running across the red brick wall behind the espresso machine, a fat sack of money in his hand. The same college guys are still playing Dungeons and Dragons at the corner table.

I feel like I'm home.

Alistair nudges my foot with the toe of his high-top Converse sneaker. "She's right. You look smug."

Smug? "I'm just happy."

"No one is that happy." Marisol stabs her needle through the stretched white fabric, adding a stitch to the bride's yellow hair.

"Especially not you," Alistair says.

Um, what?

"Well, I'm definitely less happy now then I was a minute ago," I say, frowning.

"I didn't mean anything by it," Alistair says. "You're just not acting like yourself. You're off your game. And you're never off your game."

I can't exactly argue with him about that. Okay, maybe I am still thinking about my parents and the move. I'm not sure what I've told Alistair and Marisol about what's happening, and honestly, I don't want to ruin this time with them by having a breakdown. Also, I haven't played Catan in months, so I'm a bit rusty. I've been making dumb moves. Alistair is leading by three points and Marisol is only one point behind me. Not a good look, especially since the Catan competition is in two weeks. Apparently, all three of us have signed up.

Forty minutes later, Alistair wins the first game. He stands up to stretch, arms above his head, his *Aliens* T-shirt rising just enough to show off a slice of his flat stomach. I'm suddenly warm all over. "I'm going to get a victory cookie," he says.

"Do you think Violet's going to show up?" Marisol asks me, once he's walked away.

I shrug. "She said she was coming."

"Seems like she's doing okay." She sweeps her hand across the game board and begins to separate our game pieces into colored piles.

"Define *okay*," I say. "She was pretty upset at work earlier. Sounds like she wasn't expecting Avery to dump her."

Marisol chews her lip. "Yeah. I guess that would be hard."

My thoughts circle back to my parents. My dad hasn't said much about anything, so I have no idea who made the decision to divorce. I wish I knew what happened over the past six months to change their relationship so drastically. I can't even talk to my mom about it because she's "living in the moment" at some New Agey spa retreat in Palm Springs that doesn't allow cell phones.

I have to find a way to fix this. I can't let my parents split up.

Alistair returns with a plate of cookies. He sets it down beside the game board. "Chocolate chip, fresh out of the oven," he says. "It appears that we're all winners today."

He plunks back down in the club chair beside me, just as Violet bursts through the door.

"Sorry I'm late." She takes the seat next to Marisol. She's wearing jean overalls with checkerboard Vans, her purple-streaked hair brushing her shoulders.

"Well, we're glad you did," Alistair says.

Violet picks up a cookie. "So, how do you play this game, exactly?"

Alistair goes over the rules of Catan with her. Marisol and I chime in occasionally with instructions. Catan's a tricky game to learn—it took me an hour to figure it all out—but Violet insists that we only have to walk her through it once.

"Got it," she says.

Marisol shakes her head. "There's no way you picked up all the rules that quickly."

"I'm a fast learner. It's my superpower," Violet says, lining up her orange game pieces neatly in front of her.

It turns out she's not kidding. I think she must be a Catan prodigy or something, because she's a serious competitor, right from the start.

Alistair narrows his eyes. "Are you sure you haven't played this before?" he asks when Violet snags the largest army card—and two extra points. Somehow, she's already leading the game.

"I told you—I pick things up quickly." Violet trades three blue ore cards and two yellow grain cards with the bank, in exchange for another city. "This is a pretty fun game, but I still don't get why you guys are so obsessed with it."

"We're not obsessed," Marisol says. She sounds snippy, which isn't like her at all. When I look closely at her, I notice the purple bags under her eyes.

"Uh, yeah we are." Alistair rolls the dice. Seven—the robber. We all sigh and hand half of our resource cards back to the bank.

"You should enter the Catan competition with us," I say to Violet.

Marisol glares at me.

What? I mouth back, confused.

I'm definitely picking up a hostile vibe here. The death stare she's giving me obviously means that she doesn't want Violet to play with us in the tournament. I know it can't be because Marisol sees her as competition—she's the first to admit that she just plays for fun, which is good because she pretty much sucks—so it must mean that, for some reason, she doesn't want Violet spending any more time with us.

"I'll think about it." Violet swaps her orange settlement out for her new city, a total boss move that puts her another two points ahead.

Old me probably wouldn't have extended the invitation to Violet, but that girl is gone. Or mostly gone. I've decided that this fresh start is a chance for me to be a better person. The kind of girl who helps her friend get over her broken heart.

It's my turn. I roll an eight and frown. Violet and Alistair have settlements on eight, which gives them each another ore card, the exact card I need to turn this game around. Maybe I can convince Alistair to trade with me.

"Avery isn't into board games," Violet says, grabbing another cookie. "She'd rather play mind games."

"Come on," Alistair says. "I know you're upset right now, but Avery's not like that."

"Oh yeah? Then why won't she just tell me who she dumped me for?"

Alistair holds up his hands. "You'll have to talk to her about that."

Violet leaps forward. "What does that mean? What do you know?" Her voice travels up in pitch.

He scrubs his hand through his curly sheepdog hair in frustration. "It means that I'm friends with both of you. And I want it to stay that way, so I'm keeping out of it."

Violet's eyes narrow. "I'm going to find out who it is, sooner or later, so you might as well tell me."

Alistair shakes his head.

Violet turns to Marisol. "Why is your boyfriend being such a jerk?"

I straighten, a cold feeling settling over me. Wait, what did she just say?

Alistair and Marisol aren't looking at each other, but they're both blushing hard.

My stomach drops.

Alistair isn't my boyfriend. He's Marisol's.

CHAPTER 9

Everything is a mess and life is the worst.

I can't even properly react to the news that Alistair and Marisol are together, because this is not supposed to be news to me. I'm already supposed to know about them. I'm supposed to know and be *happy* for them.

Oh my God, how did this even happen? Marisol has never had feelings for Alistair. Not that she shared with me, anyway. Or . . . maybe she did. Maybe this was all okay with the me they've been hanging around with for the past six months. Maybe that me didn't care that they were dating.

But this me cares. This me cares very much!

This is almost as bad as my parents' divorce.

"Are you all right, Em?" Alistair asks, his brow wrinkling with concern.

I shake my head. It's too hot in here and I'm sweating, which makes total sense because I'm in hell.

What happened to quoting from *The Notebook* to tell me that he could be whoever I needed him to be, if only I'd give him a chance? What happened to his feelings for me? Where did they go?

I turned my life upside down for Alistair. I thought that stupid rock would guarantee that we'd end up together, but somehow it's all gone horribly wrong. Now, not only am I going to have to start splitting my time between my parents' houses, but I don't even have Alistair to dry my tears.

"I'm not feeling so great," I say. I want to go home, crawl under the covers, and stay there forever.

"Do you want me to take you home?" he asks.

I know he's only being nice—he's being a friend—but I can't handle his concern right now. And I really don't want to be alone with him. I don't trust that I won't break down and tell him everything.

Violet saves me by offering to take me home instead. "I'm passing by your house anyway," she says.

We leave Bonus Round without even finishing our game. Violet would have won, but she forfeits to drive me home. This is the first time that I've left a game before it ended—of course, it helps that I was losing.

Violet stops at the curb in front of a vintage yellow scooter, the kind I'd probably be zipping around on if I was still going to Italy. She lifts up the black leather seat and pulls out two white helmets from the storage trunk.

I take a deep breath. I'm already feeling a tiny bit better, outside in the fresh air, although I'm nervous about doubling on her scooter. I've never ridden one before. That I remember, anyway.

This not knowing what I've done or what's happened to me over the past half a year really sucks.

Violet hands one of the helmets to me. "Are you going to tell me what that was all about?"

"It's nothing. I'm just not feeling well."

"Em, this is me you're talking to. I can tell when something's bothering you."

Okay, so Violet and I are closer than I thought. We're actual friends. I wish I could tell her everything, but I don't think she'd believe me if I told her the truth. I mean, who would? It sounds crazy. Because it is crazy.

Violet plunks her helmet on, snapping the strap into place underneath her chin. "You said you didn't care that they were dating."

So, we've talked about this before.

I can't meet her eyes. I don't know what I told her in the past, but I am definitely not okay with Alistair being with any-one other than me. My heart will never be okay with that. And I'm about to lose what little cool I have left, right here on the sidewalk.

"I know it's weird, seeing them together," she says, throwing a leg over her scooter. "But it's only been a few days. Things will settle down and you'll get used to it."

I seriously doubt that.

I sit down behind Violet and slide my arms around her waist. And even though I don't remember ever being on this scooter with her before, my muscles seem to know what to do. I hang on to her as she pulls into traffic, the wind drying the tears on my cheeks.

* * *

Maybe I should have taken the palm reader's warning a little more seriously before I stuck that crystal under my pillow. I thought a do-over would give me my friends back—and it has—but I also thought it would mean that I'd be with Alistair. No Ben, no Jiya. No one standing between us.

Least of all my best friend.

It's been two days since I found out Marisol and Alistair are together and I'm still trying to catch my breath. I haven't seen either of them since then because I've been stuck on this DIY bathroom renovation with my dad. He's taken a few days off work to do this—apparently, he got a really great sales job months ago (yay!)—but he's still not a whole lot handier than he was before (boo).

I thought that helping him might be a good distraction—and a chance to dig a little more into what tore my parents apart—but, as it turns out, retiling a shower takes forever and I was over it after five minutes. It just isn't that much fun. Especially when you don't have the first clue how to use a caulking gun.

"Emelia, you really need to pay more attention," Dad says, checking out my progress. Grouting the tile is the last step in the process—*grout* being the gooey white paste that fills the gaps between the ocean-blue tiles that, apparently, I picked out myself. "The lines are all uneven."

Okay, so he's not the only one who isn't particularly handy. My grout job is pretty sloppy, but it's hard to keep my hand steady, and also, we've been working all afternoon, no breaks, and all I can think about is what Alistair and Marisol are doing right now.

Maybe they're kissing.

God, I don't want to think about them kissing.

Plus, I haven't been able to squeeze any information out of my dad about what's going on with my mom. This afternoon has pretty much been a total bust and I'm definitely not in the mood to be scolded. My dad's complaint just pushes me over the edge, and I shove the caulking gun at him. If he's so particular, let him do it himself.

I step out of the shower and push past him. I don't want to do this anymore. I'll have to find another way to distract myself. One that doesn't involve being stuck in this sweaty bathroom.

"Emelia, come back here," Dad calls as I walk down the hall. "You can't just quit in the middle of the job."

Oh yeah? Watch me.

He follows me downstairs and into the kitchen, still holding the caulking gun. The front of his Black Sabbath T-shirt is covered in white dust from the many hours we spent chiseling off all the old, yellowing tile yesterday.

I wash the sticky caulk off my hands in the sink. Napoleon nudges my leg, reminding me we forgot to take a lunch break.

Dad takes a deep breath. "Honey, it was just a little constructive criticism—"

"If you think you can do a better job, then go right ahead," I say.

I know it's not fair to take my terrible mood out on my dad. If there's anyone I should be blaming, it's myself—I'm the one responsible for this flipped reality, after all. As far as Dad knows, I was totally on board and super eager to take on this project. Which does not sound like me, but I guess I've changed over the past six months.

"Your mom is going to be home soon," Dad says as I dry my hands on the blue gingham towel hanging from the oven. I grab the bag of dog kibble from the pantry and dump some into Napoleon's bowl. "We need to finish this up before she comes back, and I need your help to do that. The O'Malleys are a team, remember?"

Well, we used to be. I don't know if it still counts if my parents want to turn in their jerseys.

I never should have messed with that crystal. Now I can never be with Alistair, my parents have broken up, we're selling our house, and I'm stuck working on this stupid bathroom project.

My lip trembles. I've ruined everything.

✳ CHAPTER ✳
10

"So, I think that I'm going to apply to film school," Alistair says. We're leaning against the chain-link fence, watching his dog, Bitsy—a Pomeranian—chase Napoleon around the perimeter of the dog park. Alistair having a dog is another something new—apparently, he inherited her from his grandmother when she died a few months ago.

I almost said no when he texted to ask if I wanted to meet up, but I figured that I'd have to face him sometime. I thought it might be slightly less painful to be alone with him, instead of third-wheeling it with him and Marisol, but as it turns out, I was wrong. Being alone with him is super painful. Like, dagger-in-the-heart painful.

"Makes sense," I say. It isn't exactly surprising that he wants to go to film school. He's been talking about it for years.

Alistair shrugs. "USC is pretty hard to get into, though. And super expensive."

I suck in a breath. USC is a million miles away. I just got him back in my life and now he's planning to move to California? And, okay, I'm moving too, and college is still a year away, but it's scary to think that there's going to be distance between us again—even if it's a physical separation rather than an emotional one.

It's hard to hide my feelings about all of this, but I'm trying. I think I'm failing, though, because Alistair keeps shooting worried looks at me when he thinks I'm not paying attention. It's not just the fact that he's potentially going to move away, though, that has me down. It's everything.

So, here's what I've managed to piece together about my life after carefully reading through six months of text messages: Alistair, Marisol, and I never went to Ben's party. Which means that Ben and I never made out. Which means that he never asked me to the winter formal, never asked me to be his girlfriend. I was his lab partner, nothing more, and that seems to have come to an end months ago.

Without the threat of another guy hovering around me, Alistair never confessed his feelings for me. And I never gathered the courage to tell him how I felt about him, either—although maybe that's because I never really realized how I felt about Alistair until I'd already chosen Ben.

And somehow, he ended up with Marisol instead.

"I'm sure you could get a scholarship." I squeeze Napoleon's red rubber ball in my hand, taking out my aggression on my dog's favorite toy.

Alistair sighs. "Yeah, maybe," he says, squinting up at the

sun. He pulls a pair of aviator sunglasses out of the pocket of his frayed jean vest and slides them on. "I have to submit a video as part of my application."

"Oh yeah?"

Squeeze, squeeze, squeeze.

"I think I'm going to do a short documentary about the Catan competition," he says.

"Good idea."

I know I should be more excited for him—he deserves more than clipped answers—but my bad mood has taken an even sharper downturn. I'm mad that things haven't worked out like they were supposed to. Mad that he chose Marisol, when he had feelings for me. And, okay, I know that makes me a huge hypocrite—I chose Ben over him, after all—but I can't help it. Alistair doesn't know the great lengths I've gone to in order to be here with him.

Squeeze, squeeze, squeeze.

"Em, are you all right?"

"Why does everyone keep asking me that?" I snap. I bring my arm back and pitch Napoleon's ball into the field. Two golden retrievers speed toward it, narrowly missing running into each other.

"Uh, because we're worried about you," Alistair replies. "You seem pretty wound up, and you've been avoiding me for days. What's that about?"

If only I could tell him. My shoulders sag. None of this is Alistair's fault. It's mine. We're in this situation because I didn't make the right choice in the first place.

"I'm fine," I say. "I just . . . have a lot on my mind lately. Sorry."

"You want to talk about it?"

"I wouldn't even know where to begin," I say.

"Start at the very beginning . . . I hear it's a very good place to start."

I roll my eyes. "You're not going to sing, are you?"

"Would it get you to talk?" He smiles and my heart skips. I wish I'd paid more attention to how he made me feel when I had the chance.

The gate to the dog park squeaks open. A tall blond girl in jean cutoffs and a cropped pink T-shirt enters the park with a Jack Russell terrier. She spots us and walks over.

"Hey," she says, bending down to unhook her dog from its pink leash. "I was hoping I'd run into you guys here."

I stare blankly at her. I have no idea who this girl is. She doesn't look the least bit familiar, but from the easy smile she gives me, it's seems that she knows me.

"I thought you were working today," Alistair says.

She shrugs. "I was supposed to, but I switched my shift. Violet's on the schedule, and I thought it would be better if we didn't work together for a while. I thought she might need some space."

Ah. This must be Avery. Violet's ex.

Alistair shakes his head. "Space isn't going to help. You really need to straighten things out with her."

"I've tried," she says. "She's not answering my texts."

"Then you should try harder."

I glance at him. Why is he pushing her on this, when it isn't really any of his business?

Avery bristles. "Look, I know this is an inconvenience for you—"

Alistair glares at her, and whatever she was going to say next is lost in his silent warning. Her eyes flick to me and a blush starts to creep across her cheeks.

Hmm.

"I'm just saying . . . Violet made it pretty clear she doesn't want to talk to me right now, and I have to respect that," she says. "I feel really bad about how everything went down with her. I know I didn't handle things well. I wish I could go back and do it all differently, but I don't have a time machine."

Or a magic, time-turning crystal.

I stiffen. Wait. Maybe I can use the crystal to fix things with my parents and with Alistair.

Maybe what I need is a do-over of my do-over.

A tiny shiver goes through me. I know the palm reader said that the crystal was a one-shot deal and there was no going back, but what if she was wrong? What if I *can* change things up again?

I bite my lip. What if I could do my life a million times over, until I got it right?

"It might help if you told her the truth," Alistair says to Avery.

"Al. You know I can't do that."

Violet was right—Avery must be seeing someone else. And Alistair clearly knows who that someone is. I wonder, though, why Avery thinks it's better to keep it a secret than to tell Violet. I get that she probably doesn't want to hurt her even more than she already has, but lying about moving on isn't going to help the situation.

"I'm hoping she'll come around," Avery says. "I'd like to be friends again."

I almost smile. Avery's kidding herself. I may not know Violet well, but I do know that the girl can hold a grudge. I very much doubt that she'll be eager to be friends anytime soon. The most Avery should hope for is polite indifference.

But none of this is any of my business. And I'm not sure why Alistair is making it his. Sure, he's Violet's friend and he's probably feeling protective of her, but this is really between her and Avery.

"I guess time will tell," Alistair says.

Time. It makes me wonder if my do-over somehow affected Violet and Avery's relationship. It seems to have changed things for the people around me—my parents are splitting up; Alistair and Marisol are together. I know the palm reader warned me that if you change one thing about the past, you change everything about the future, but I thought she just meant my future. I didn't realize my choice would affect everyone around me as well.

I frown. I hate that I've screwed things up for my family and friends, but I'm sure I can fix it. I can fix all of it.

I'm going to make sure that we all get a happy ending.

✴ CHAPTER ✴
11

That night, I put the crystal under my pillow again, but I'm so excited that I have a hard time getting to sleep. I wake up a bunch of times, and each time, I turn on my bedside lamp to see if my room looks any different. But it never does.

Finally I drift into a heavy sleep. So heavy, in fact, that I don't wake up until almost nine o'clock the next morning. I sit up, frowning as I glance around my room. It looks exactly the same as last night—the same purple walls, the same yellow hoodie hanging from the back of my desk chair, the same glass of water on my nightstand. I look down at my pajamas.

Same cat-astronaut pj's.

I sigh and pull the crystal out from underneath my pillow. I guess I shouldn't have gotten my hopes up. After all, the palm reader did say that the crystal was a one-time-only thing. I just so badly wanted it to change my life again.

Now what am I going to do?

Napoleon pushes my door open and wanders in, his tongue hanging out of his mouth. I can hear Dad banging around in the bathroom down the hall, already working on the renovation.

I set the crystal on my nightstand and climb out of bed. I give my dog a quick scratch behind the ears before leaving my room.

"Hi, kid," Dad says. He's spreading a plastic drop cloth over the tile floor. A can of the silvery blue paint we picked out together at Castle Hardware the other day is sitting on the counter, along with an assortment of paintbrushes. Thick green masking tape runs in a neat line around the perimeter of the room as well as the ceiling.

"What's the tape for?" I ask him.

"It's so that we don't get paint where we're not supposed to," he says. He straightens the cloth and then uses a screwdriver to pry the metal lid off the paint can. The paint looks a little less blue and a little more shimmery silver than I remember it.

"You should change," Dad says. "You don't want to get paint on your pajamas."

I frown. "But I haven't even had breakfast yet."

He shrugs. "Not my fault you slept in."

"Daaaaad."

"Emeeeeelia."

I roll my eyes. "Ugh, fine. Just give me a minute."

I go back into my bedroom and change out of my pj's and into a pair of cutoffs and an old T-shirt. Before I leave my room again, I check my phone. I know that my mom isn't supposed to have any communication with us while she's at this wellness retreat, but I've been hoping that she'd make an exception and respond if she saw my increasingly desperate messages. Still there's nothing from her.

I scowl. This sucks. I've made a mess of everything, and without the crystal, I don't have any idea how to fix my parents' relationship or how to be okay with Alistair not being my boyfriend. And on top of all that, I have to help my dad paint the bathroom. This day is just the worst.

My eye catches on the crystal on my nightstand and a thought occurs to me. The palm reader said that this crystal would only work once—but she didn't say anything about using *another* crystal . . .

I smile. Maybe I just need to go back to the night market and buy another one.

✳ ✳ ✳

That evening, I'm the first person through the gates when the night market opens. I speed past the food booths, the carnival games, the Ferris wheel. The crystal is nestled in my palm, my fingers wrapped protectively around it. I brought it to show the palm reader. I want to make sure that she sells me the exact same type of crystal with magical time-turning abilities—especially because she won't remember having sold it to me in the first place.

Just up ahead, I spot the picnic table where I sat with Ben and his friends. And there's the spot where I saw Alistair and Jiya kissing. The weight of that memory sits on my chest. I turn, following the path I took that night, toward the dark corner of the market and the palm reader's purple tent.

My breath starts to quicken. This area of the night market is made up of vendors selling cell phone cases, novelty T-shirts, and costume jewelry. The air smells like cinnamon doughnuts. Somewhere, a busker is playing "Blackbird" on his guitar.

I come to the chain-link fence that marks the end of the night market.

Wait. Where's the palm reader's tent?

I turn in a circle, frantic. This was the spot, I'm sure of it. But there's nothing but an empty space where the tent used to be.

I run a hand through my hair. Okay, maybe all is not lost—maybe they just moved the palm reader's tent to a different location.

I approach a booth cluttered with classic-rock posters and yellow plastic crates of records. A guy with a shag haircut is behind the booth, thumbing through a stack of old *Rolling Stone* magazines.

"Excuse me," I ask him. "Do you know what happened to the palm reader who was here earlier this week?"

He glances at me, confused. "There was a palm reader here?"

"She was in the purple tent," I say. "She sold crystals and read tarot cards?"

He shrugs. "No idea."

Great.

I'm about to walk around and see if I can find her, when my phone beeps. It's Violet.

What are you doing right this second?

At the night market, I reply.

With who?

With myself.

Why?

I can't tell her the real reason, obvi.

I'm grabbing some dinner.

Well, bring it over! I'm bored.

A few seconds later, my phone beeps again.

Can you get me a tornado potato?

I wander around the night market, still searching for the palm reader's tent, but if it's here, I don't see it. I ask a few other vendors, but no one seems to even remember it, which is totally weird.

I finally remember that the night market lists all its vendors on its website. I pull up the site on my phone and scroll through the list, but the palm reader isn't on it.

I sigh heavily. I don't know what to make of that. Maybe she was only here for one night? Or maybe, in this reality, she was never at the night market at all.

Either way, she's obviously not here now, so I might as well get Violet's potato and go over to her house. I'll have to think about how I'm going to track the palm reader down later.

I find the tornado potato booth. There's a sign of a cartoon potato dancing, salt and pepper raining down on its head. I'm waiting for my order when I hear a familiar voice just behind me.

"One of these places has burgers made with doughnuts," Ben says.

My breath catches. I haven't seen him since I used the crystal, although he has crossed my mind. How could he not? He wasn't always a jerk—not at first, anyway.

I've wondered what this moment would be like, but you can never really be prepared to run into an ex. Although I guess it shouldn't be a surprise that he's here—it's pretty much his favorite place.

"Gross," says another familiar voice. "You're going to clog all your arteries if you keeping eating junk like that."

My eyes widen. Olivia.

My first instinct is to run away before they notice me—forget about the stupid potatoes—but then I remember that I don't need to avoid him. There was no bad breakup—no breakup at all, in fact. As far as Ben knows, I was his lab partner and nothing more. A girl he might have been briefly interested in, who never showed up to one of his parties. End of story.

Still, this is super awkward. There may be no reason to avoid Ben, but hearing his voice has set some feelings off in me that I don't quite know what to do with.

I really hope he doesn't notice me.

"Emelia?"

Okay, so I guess pretending to be invisible doesn't work. I briefly close my eyes and then turn around, pasting a friendly smile on my face.

"Oh, hey," I say.

Ben smiles. "I thought that was you."

"Well. You thought right." I laugh, but it sounds so fake that I actually cringe. I glance over my shoulder at the booth, silently begging the potato guy to hurry up with my order.

"It's your hair," Ben says. "You know, it kind of looks like a sunset."

I nod. "I've been told that before."

By you, actually.

"Hi, Olivia," I say.

She smiles tightly. My eyes catch on their hands, their fingers laced together, and my mouth goes dry.

Ben and Olivia are holding hands.

So, that's a plot twist I didn't see coming. Olivia and Drew have been together since freshman year. He's Ben's best friend—or was, anyway. I wonder what Ben dating Olivia means for their friendship.

"This line is ridiculous," Olivia mutters.

"The potatoes are totally worth it, trust me," Ben says, slinging his arm around her shoulders. He leans forward and gives her a kiss on the cheek.

I narrow my eyes. Ben wasn't super into public displays of affection when we were together. I could barely get him to hold my hand.

They start to make out, so there's no need to wish I was invisible anymore—they've already forgotten about me. *Which is what I wanted,* I remind myself, turning back around.

CHAPTER

12

I have to do a search for Violet's address because I have no idea where she lives and I can't exactly ask her, since I'm supposed to have been there plenty of times before. So I'm not entirely sure that I've got the right house until Mrs. Chen opens the door. At least, I think it's Mrs. Chen. She looks an awful lot like Violet, except her hair isn't purple, and she's mom age.

"Emelia, hi," she says. "It's so lovely to see you."

I take a chance. "Hi, Mrs. Chen."

She eyes the potatoes I'm holding in front of me like lances, and smiles. These potatoes better be excellent, for all the trouble I've gone through to get them here. I had to stash them in the basket of my bicycle.

"Violet's favorite," she says. "Hopefully you have more luck getting her to eat than I have." She steps back and holds the door open to let me inside. "She's up in her room. I can't seem to get her out of there these days." She sighs and shakes her head. "I'm really glad that she has a friend like you, especially now that things have gone sideways with Avery."

"Mom!" Violet bellows from somewhere upstairs. "I can hear you! Stop discussing my personal life with Emelia!"

"Oh, you can hear me now, but you can't hear me when I call for you to come down and load the dishwasher?" Mrs. Chen says, rolling her eyes.

Silence.

Mrs. Chen sighs again.

I walk up the stairs of their artfully decorated split-level house, pausing when I get to the top. I hope Mrs. Chen isn't watching me, because I'm not sure which room is Violet's.

I find Violet in the last room on the left. She's sitting on a super girly white daybed—definitely not the kind of furniture I would have pictured her owning. She's wearing a plastic shower cap over her hair. Her room reeks of peroxide, burning the inside of my nose.

"Hey," she says.

I hand her a potato.

"It's probably cold," I say.

"I like them better cold," she says. "And speaking of . . ." She points to her shower cap. "I'm dyeing it blond. Avery called me an ice queen once, and I figured the outside might as well match the inside."

"I'm sure she didn't mean it."

Violet shrugs. "She did. But I've been thinking about it,

and maybe she's not wrong. I know I can be a little standoffish sometimes."

"You're not standoffish . . . you just like to keep to yourself."

She gives me a small smile. "It sounds nicer when you say it that way."

Something small and brown suddenly scuttles over my feet and darts under the bed. I let out a scream.

"Sorry, I should have told you that Paul's out of his cage," Violet says, taking a small bite of her potato. I sit down beside her on the bed, pulling my feet up so that Paul can't run over them again with his creepy little paws.

Violet sighs heavily. "Anyway, I've been thinking about Avery—all I do is think about Avery—and how I messed everything up," she says. "I realized that it's my fault she dumped me. I drove her away with my ice-cold ways."

I think about how I ran into Avery this morning at the dog park. I briefly wonder if I should tell Violet that I saw her, but then just as quickly decide against it. Violet will definitely want me to tell her what we talked about. She's already depressed, so what good would it do her to hear that Avery is definitely keeping something from her.

"I wish I could do it all differently, you know?" she says.

Boy, do I ever.

I should tell her to be careful what you wish for.

We sit in silence, eating our potatoes, listening to Paul scrabble around underneath Violet's bed. I glance around her room. Everything about it seems so un-Violet that it almost makes me laugh. From the dainty white furniture to the ballerina-pink shade on her walls. She has a bunch of hand-drawn posters of Disney villains—Ursula, Maleficent, the Evil Queen. They're amazingly detailed, almost professional, and I want to ask her if she drew these pictures herself, but those are new-friend questions, and from what I can gather, we're past that point in our friendship.

The only thing that even remotely seems like Violet in this entire room is the oval-framed embroidery mounted above her bed—a cute red fox nestled between *For* and *Sake*.

For Fox's Sake.

I'm pretty sure it's one of Marisol's.

Violet catches me looking at it. "Avery gave it to me for my birthday. Miraculously, my mom somehow still hasn't figured out what it means."

We finish picking the last of the potatoes off the skewers. Violet stands up and tosses them into her garbage can. She's wearing long army-green shorts that reach past her knees and a black T-shirt over a long-sleeve white T-shirt. Very early-nineties Seattle grunge-rocker. Her main style influence seems to be Kurt Cobain.

My fingers are covered in orange cheese powder. I duck into the bathroom across the hall from her room to wash my hands. By the time I get back, Violet is holding a small brown-and-white hedgehog.

Paul gazes at me with little black beady eyes, his tiny black nose twitching, and he's not creepy at all. My heart explodes.

"Here." Violet gives him to me. I don't have the first clue how to hold a hedgehog, but Paul settles right in the palm of my hand. He's lying on his back, his soft white belly exposed, four tiny pink feet splayed up in the air.

Violet walks over to the antique mirror hanging above her dresser and lifts up her shower cap. She checks her roots and frowns.

"Avery is my person," she says. "I know how that sounds—I mean, we're still in high school. It's ridiculous to think that we can last forever. But I can't help it. I really feel like she's the one."

"Maybe you should talk to her." Paul squirms in my hand. His quills aren't as sharp as I expected them to be.

"I can't! It's too hard," she says. "Besides, I'd rather show her how I'm feeling than tell her."

"That sounds a lot harder than just talking to her."

She lets out a breath. "Maybe. But it has more impact. And if I'm going to win her back, I need a grand gesture."

Violet seems confident that this will fix everything with Avery, but I'm not so sure. It didn't work for Alistair. He showed up at my house, quoting *The Notebook*, wearing his heart on his sleeve, and I still turned him down.

My throat closes. I can't imagine how he felt when I turned him down. I guess that's one reason to be glad that the crystal worked—he won't have to carry that awful memory around.

And then there's the little issue of Avery seeing someone else.

"Okay, but what if . . . ," I start.

"What if what?"

How to put this delicately, in a way that won't cause her

to lose her shit? I know what it's like to be torn between two people, and I don't want Violet to put herself out there and get even more hurt.

"What if she's already moved on?" I say.

Violet narrows her eyes. "What do you know?"

"Nothing. I swear. I just think you should be cautious, that's all."

"Being cautious isn't going to get Avery to come back to me," she says.

A grand gesture might not do that, either.

Paul is starting to get squirmy. Violet gestures to his metal cage in the corner of her room. I set him gently inside, on top of the wood shavings, and close the door.

"Maybe you can find out who she is," she says.

What?

"Would that really make you feel better?" I say.

She shrugs. "Information is power. If I know who I'm up against, then maybe I can level the playing field. Right now, I'm not even in the game."

I feel uneasy. Violet is my friend, but Avery is too, apparently, and I don't want to put myself in the middle of this. Even though it already feels like I'm in the middle of it.

"I'll see what I can find out," I say reluctantly. Maybe I'm being too cynical. Maybe everything will work out for her.

"Great! And you have to help me think of something monumental to do for her," Violet says. "Something that will totally blow her mind."

She checks her roots in the mirror again. "I have to go wash this out," she says. She pauses in her doorway, studying me thoughtfully. "You know, I think we should take a few more inches off your hair. You could totally pull off a short bob."

I stare at her. I didn't realize that Violet was responsible for my new haircut. I wonder how she talked me into it.

"Nope, I'm good, thanks," I say. I can barely pull what's left of my hair into a ponytail—there's no way I'm letting her near my head with scissors again.

* * *

"What about this one?" Dad asks the next afternoon, holding up a shower curtain featuring cartoon sea turtles wearing sunglasses. His fingers are speckled with silvery-blue paint. We'd hardly finished putting the first coat on the bathroom when he insisted that we run out and get a bunch of accessories.

"It doesn't go with anything else we've chosen." Plus, I hate it. I mean, why are the turtles even wearing sunglasses? It doesn't make any sense.

"But it's blue. It matches the walls." He sticks the shower curtain into our shopping cart.

I roll my eyes. It does not match the walls, and why is he even bothering to ask my opinion when he's already made up his mind?

"Now we just need to find a new light fixture." He pushes the cart down the aisle and disappears around the corner. We've been at Castle Hardware for fifteen minutes, but I haven't seen

Alistair yet. I know he's working today because I checked his schedule, like a total stalker.

As I round the corner to follow my dad, I spot Alistair in the paint section, mixing up a can of paint in the shaker. I should probably stick with my dad—who knows what kind of ugly light fixture he'll pick if he's left unsupervised?—but my heart leads my feet in another direction.

Alistair glances up as I approach. He smiles and makes me wish, for the millionth time, that everything wasn't so complicated.

"Hey," I say.

"What are you doing in here on your day off?" he asks as the shaker stops. He removes the paint can from the machine.

"Just picking up a few things with my dad for the bathroom."

"Right. The bathroom reno. How's that going?"

I shrug. "We haven't killed each other yet," I say.

"You guys need any help? I could come by after my shift ends." Alistair pops the lid off the paint can, dips a small brush inside, then paints a streak of lavender across the top of the lid so the customer will know the exact shade of the color inside.

I shake my head. "Thanks, but I think we're almost finished."

I'm trying to avoid any more one-on-one time with him, but it's not easy to do, especially because spending time with him is exactly what I want most. God, doing the right thing is hard.

"I guess I'll see you at Marisol's later, then," he says. We're heading over there tonight to watch a movie. I haven't seen her since I ran out of Bonus Round, and she's barely answering my texts, which is super weird and concerning.

"Is she mad at me?" I ask him.

"I don't think so."

"You don't think so?" That means she is.

"What would she be mad at you for?" he asks.

Um, I don't know . . . maybe because she knows I have a thing for her boyfriend? Not that I'm going to tell him that.

Alistair sighs. "Em, she wouldn't invite you over if she was upset with you."

Or she would *invite me over so that she could chew me out in person.*

"You're taking this too personally. She's just got a lot going on right now," he adds.

"You keep saying that."

"That's because it's true," he says. "I've barely seen her, either."

That does make me feel better, because if they're not hanging out, then it means they're not making out.

Suddenly I hear my dad yelling my name across the store.

I wince. "I'd better go."

"See you tonight," Alistair says.

I walk over to the lighting aisle. My dad's holding up a cheap-looking light fixture—a plain brass bar with three spots to screw in light bulbs. It's not that different from the light fixture we just took down.

"How about this one?" he asks. "It's on sale."

"How about something like this instead?" I point to a fixture with three simple silver shades, shaped like bells. It's not on sale, but with my employee discount, it shouldn't cost too much more than the other one.

Dad shrugs. "Yeah, okay."

He pulls the box off the shelf and places it in the cart. Now I just have to talk him out of the sea-turtle shower curtain. Although, maybe I'm approaching this whole reno wrong—maybe I should be making the bathroom as ugly as possible so no one will want to buy the house.

✳ CHAPTER ✳
13

"I really don't get why you're so obsessed with this movie," I say, picking up the battered DVD case of *Weekend at Bernie's*, this ridiculous film from the eighties about two guys who carry their dead boss around, pretending that he's still alive, so they can continue to party at his beach house.

"What kind of a host invites you to his house for the weekend and dies on you?" Alistair quotes.

"I can't do it," I say, grabbing the DVD from his hands and stuffing it back on the shelf. "I would literally rather watch anything else."

We spend a lot of time in Marisol's basement because her parents are the least likely to bother us. But since Marisol doesn't have cable, our choices for movies are pretty limited. She doesn't have Netflix, either. I mean, what century are we even living in? If there's something that we're really dying to see, Alistair or I will hook up a phone to her TV, but most of the time we just pick something from her parents' extensive—and ancient—DVD collection. They used to own a video store, back when video stores were actually a thing, so they have approximately a billion DVDs. And yet, somehow, we always end up watching the same movies.

Hanging out with them together isn't as stressful as I expected it to be. Sure, no one wants to be a third wheel—especially when one of those wheels is the boy you're crazy about—but so far it feels like old times. Alistair and Marisol are not all over each other, as I feared they would be.

And this is all temporary, anyway, until I find the palm reader and get my hands on another crystal.

"How about *Moulin Rouge*?" I suggest.

Alistair's eyebrows gather together. "Uh, you talked me into watching that a few weeks ago. You don't remember?"

"Oh. Right." My cheeks start to burn. It's way too easy to trip over details about your life when you have no idea what's happened in it.

"How about *The Princess Bride*?" Yes, we've watched it a million times, but that makes it a safe bet.

Alistair smiles. "My name is Inigo Montoya. You killed my father. Prepare to die."

I'll take that as a yes. I grab the DVD from the shelf and turn to look at Marisol. She's sitting on the couch, stitching a tiny cactus onto a pocket square. For some inexplicable reason, the cactus is wearing a cowboy hat. She lets out a frustrated moan and throws the hoop onto the coffee table.

"Ugh. I'm never going to finish all these orders. Why did I think an Etsy boutique was a good idea?" she says.

A flash of guilt goes through me. Apparently, I'm the one who encouraged her to open the Etsy shop in the first place.

"Maybe we can help you," Alistair says.

She snorts. "Yeah, that's great, Al. All those hours you've spent learning to embroider are really going to help me out." She lets out a breath and rubs her eyes. Several of her fingertips are covered in bandages. "Sorry. I'm just sick of spending every waking moment doing this. I thought it would be a fun summer job, a way to make some extra money. But it's turned into a nightmare. God, I want to quit."

"So quit," Alistair says.

"I can't! I've already taken money for these stupid projects!" She wails and flops back down onto the couch face-first.

Alistair and I exchange a worried glance. I know she's exhausted and stressed, but this is so not Marisol. I feel like we're standing on the shore, watching her get sucked under the waves, when we should be throwing her a life ring.

The tension in the room is very real. I'm expecting Alistair to go over to comfort her, but he stays put beside me. Maybe he feels awkward because I'm here. I know I feel awkward that I'm here.

Alistair clears his throat. "Why don't we skip the movie," he says. "Let's go out and do something."

Marisol turns her head and glares at him. "I can't go anywhere. Didn't you hear me? I'm going to be stuck in this basement for the rest of the summer working on these orders," she says. "I'm like the farmer's daughter, locked in the dungeon. Forced to spin straw into gold or the king will cut my head off."

"I think you're talking about Rumpelstiltskin, and I'm pretty sure that's just a fairy tale," he says. "I promise, no one's going to cut your head off if you don't finish your cactus. They'd have to get through Em and me first."

Marisol buries her face in the couch cushions again.

"Come on," he cajoles. "If we watch a movie, then you're just going to keep working. We won't keep you out long. The break will do you good."

"I'll buy you a frozen mocha at Bonus Round," I say. "The Catan competition is coming up, so we really should practice."

But instead of excited acceptance, there's just dead silence.

"I'm not entering the competition," Marisol finally mumbles.

"What? Why not?" I ask.

She sits up and smooths a hand over her dark curls. "Because I suck at Catan."

"You don't suck."

"Em. I suck. I have no shot at winning."

"Since when is winning the most important thing?"

Marisol rolls her eyes. "Come off it. You don't have any idea what it feels like to lose at anything. You're living your best life."

I blink, taken aback. If she only knew.

"Actually, I'm not entering either." Alistair flashes me a guilty look. "If I'm going to film the competition for my application, then I can't play in it."

"Okay, then I'm not playing either," I say. It's not a team thing, we were all entering as individuals, so it shouldn't matter if I drop out too. To be honest, I don't really care about the competition. It was Alistair's idea to sign up in the first place.

"You have to play," he says. "I need subjects for my documentary, and I was going to focus on you and Violet."

This is news to me.

"When did I agree to this?"

He smiles sheepishly. "Right now?"

I sigh. "Fine."

Marisol's phone buzzes. She reads something on her screen, and her mood shifts as rapidly as the sun appearing from behind the clouds. Her shoulders relax and her lips even curl into a small smile.

"Um, actually," she says, without looking up from her phone. "I appreciate what you guys are trying to do, but I'm super cranky, obviously, and I think I just need to be alone for a while."

Alistair and I exchange another worry-filled glance. Neither of us wants to leave her when she's feeling this way. Especially because she'll probably just pick up her embroidery hoop again.

"I promise I'll take a break." She stands up and starts walking toward the stairs.

"Okay, well . . . if you're sure," I say, following her.

There's a strange vibe as she waits for us to slip on our sneakers. She keeps looking at her phone, and she's antsy, like she can't wait for us to leave.

There's no way I can watch her kiss Alistair goodbye—too uncomfortable and weird and heartbreaking—so I leave the house first, to give them a moment of privacy. But I guess they don't need it, because Alistair steps out right after me, and then

Marisol is closing the door and we're standing on the sidewalk, staring at each other.

"What the heck was that all about?" I say.

He shakes his head. "She's just really stressed out right now."

"Yeah, I picked up on that." If I didn't know better, from the way she rushed us out after she got that message, I'd think she was ditching us for someone. But Marisol would never do that to Alistair.

"There's just a lot going on right now," he says.

I frown. He makes it sound like it's not only the embroidery orders that are causing her to flip out. Whatever else is bothering her, it's probably information I'm supposed to know. My chest tightens. I'm sure Marisol has filled me in on everything going on in her life, but this six-month hole in my memory is making it difficult for me.

"I'll call Violet. Maybe she can meet us at Bonus Round," I say, pulling out my phone.

"She doesn't need the practice. She's like a Catan genius," Alistair says. He looks up at the stars, just beginning to flicker in the night sky. "It's a nice night. Why don't we skip Bonus Round and go for gelato instead?"

He's not looking at me, but I feel the charge in the air. My hands start to shake. I know Marisol told us to go without her, but that's only because she doesn't know how I feel about Alistair. Or that, in another life, he told me how he felt about me. And while everything else may have changed, those feelings are still there.

Stop it, I tell myself. *This isn't a date. It's just two friends, going for gelato on a perfect summer evening. Something we've done a zillion times before. Stop reading into it.*

"Okay," I say.

We're close enough to town—and Alistair's right, it is a nice night—that we decide to walk. We pass by his house, nestled behind a squat wall of shrubs, right next to Marisol's place. All the lights are out.

"My mom took Cameron on an extended camping trip," he says, gesturing to his house. "I've got the place to myself for the next two weeks."

"You didn't want to go with them?"

"Stuck in a tent in the middle of nowhere with my thirteen-year-old sister who snores like a bear? Pass."

I smile. "You're lucky. I don't think my parents would let me stay home by myself."

We walk in silence for a block. "So, what was up between you and Avery at the dog park the other day?" I ask.

"What do you mean?"

"Things were super tense between you guys. She said something about all of this being an inconvenience for you?"

Alistair stiffens. He stuffs his hands in his pockets. "I don't know."

"I think you do," I say. "You were really pushing her to tell Violet something."

"Yeah, well. I've decided it's better to just stay out of it. No good will come from getting involved."

"So you do know what's going on, then. Is Avery seeing someone else?"

"Em, it's none of my business."

"I mean, it kind of is. Violet's your friend."

Alistair sighs. "Avery's my friend too. And I promised her that I wouldn't say anything," he says. "I'm keeping my mouth shut. Trust me, it's better that way."

We reach Bella Gelato. He holds open the door and I walk inside. The shop smells like vanilla and freshly made waffle cones. By some miracle, there's not much of a line tonight—usually the place is packed.

There's a pop-up photo booth in the corner, new since the last time I was in here. I grab Alistair's arm and drag him toward it.

"Come on," I say.

I push back the curtain and Alistair squeezes into the booth with me. There's barely enough room to turn around, just one stool that we both have to perch on, and I end up practically sitting in his lap. Being this close to him makes me nervous.

I lean forward and plug in a couple of dollars. We watch the counter, waiting for the flash. The rule is we always wait until the last second before we make a face. I open my eyes wide and stick out my tongue as the light flashes. We take three more photos, each one sillier than the last, until my side hurts from laughing.

We climb out of the booth.

"Strawberry, waffle cone?" Alistair asks me.

I nod, staying behind to wait for our photos to develop. I watch Alistair out of the corner of my eye as he orders our gelato.

The photos drop into the slot. I pick them up, smiling at our ridiculousness. The last photo is my favorite—Alistair laughing, his dark curls hanging across his forehead, his eyes closed.

I tear the photo strip in half.

Alistair returns with our gelato. He waves me away when I try to give him some money.

"I've got this," he says.

I hand him his half of the photo strip. He starts to smile, but then a strange expression takes over his face. He blinks and tucks the photo into his pocket.

"You want to take a walk down to the river?" I suggest.

He nods.

My palms are sweating as we walk down the winding gravel path lit by a bunch of old-fashioned lampposts. I find a fancy scrolled-iron bench overlooking the water and sit down. Alistair settles in beside me, as if we're still in the photo booth and we need to squeeze together.

We eat our gelato in silence—unless you count the sound of my heart thundering in my ears. What am I doing? This was a bad idea. Spending time alone with Alistair isn't going to make the feelings I have for him magically disappear. If anything, it's just going to make everything worse.

I should make up an excuse and go home, stop whatever it is that's happening here in its tracks, but I don't. I remind myself that I'm not doing anything to hurt Marisol—I'm not even doing anything worth feeling guilty about. But still, I feel guilty, because I like him.

The moon reflects off the water. A couple of swans glide by, side by side, their white feathers glowing in the dim light.

"Violet thinks she can win Avery back," I say.

Alistair sighs heavily. "We're back to Violet and Avery again?"

It seems like a safe enough subject. I certainly can't tell him what I'm really thinking. Which is that I wish this really was a date.

"She wants to do something big," I say. "Like a grand gesture. Any ideas?"

If anyone can come up with something romantic, it should be Alistair. After all, this is the boy who showed up to my house at midnight to tell me how he felt about me.

He purses his lips as he digs his spoon into his gelato. "A grand gesture isn't going to win Avery back," he says. "Nothing is going to win Avery back. She's moved on. Violet's only going to embarrass herself."

But . . . Alistair loves grand gestures. I know he doesn't remember that he made one to me—to him, that moment never existed—but still, my stomach bottoms out, just thinking of how embarrassed and upset he must have been when I turned him down. I'd like to think that Avery will have more sense than I did, that she'll realize what she's losing before it's too late.

"How do you know? Maybe Avery will love it," I say. "Maybe they'll get back together."

He shakes his head. "If Violet and Avery were meant to be together, they'd still be together. There's a reason they broke up, Em. Violet just doesn't want to accept it."

"And what would that reason be, exactly?" I ask him. "Because Avery wasn't too clear with Violet about why she wanted to break up."

"I can't tell you that," he replies.

"Violet asked for my help, so I'm going to help her."

"You'd help her more if you could convince her to move on," he says.

My cheeks heat up. I take an angry bite of my waffle cone. I can feel Alistair staring at me, trying to figure out why I'm mad. I'm not sure why I'm taking his refusal to help personally, but I am.

After a minute, he says, "Why are we fighting about this, when it has nothing to do with us?" He sets his empty cup down beside him on the bench and turns to face me. "Yes, it sucks that Violet got dumped, but we don't know anything about what their relationship was really like," he says. "She may not see it now, but this could all be for the best. Things usually have a way of working out as they're supposed to."

Well, that certainly hasn't proven true for me. If things worked out as they were supposed to, Alistair and I would be together. My parents would still be together and we wouldn't be selling our house. And, who knows, Violet and Avery might even still be together.

I take a deep breath. All of this just makes me even more determined to find that palm reader—and fast.

✳ CHAPTER ✳
14

"It's crooked," I say the next afternoon, staring at the new light fixture Dad and I have just finished installing above the bathroom sink.

Dad studies the fixture. "I think it's fine," he says. "Good enough, anyway." He leans forward and wipes a smudge from the mirror we spent a good part of the morning framing. The thick whitewashed wood has a pretty obvious chip in the bottom corner. There's paint on the baseboards, and the grout between the shower tiles is sloppy. There's nothing "good enough" about this bathroom.

"What are you so worried about?" Dad asks me. "We're not even going to live here."

My chest aches. "Don't remind me."

Although maybe this sad DIY job isn't the end of the world. Maybe it will deter anyone from buying our house.

Dad puts his arm around my shoulders and squeezes. "Em,

I know this is hard," he says. "But I promise you, everything is going to be all right."

How can he promise me that?

God, if I'd never messed with the crystal, then this wouldn't even be happening. My parents would still be happy. Or maybe not quite as happy as they seem to be now, but at least they wouldn't be breaking up.

Dad picks up the seashell-covered picture frame I set on the wooden shelf above the toilet. It's a photo of the three of us in San Francisco, the Golden Gate Bridge rising behind us in the background. It was taken the last time we went on a family trip, when I was ten.

Truthfully, I brought it in here hoping it would make him nostalgic. And for a moment I think my plan worked. He stares at the photo, a small lost-in-memories smile crossing his face.

"Karen says we need to remove any personal items," he says.

I frown. Karen's our real-estate agent. I haven't met her yet—or maybe I have and I just don't have any memory of it. At any rate, apparently she's instructed us to take down everything that makes our house our home. Dad says that buyers want to be able to imagine themselves in the place.

"That goes for your room, too," he says.

I sigh heavily. He's been after me to declutter my room for days. There's no way around it, so after we're done in the bathroom, I take down my chili-pepper lights and the poster of Cuba, along with the photos of Alistair and Marisol and me on my bulletin board. Most are old photos that I remember, but there are a few that I have no memory of taking. Like the one of Marisol and me mugging in front of Bonus Round. Another of the three of us at winter formal, Alistair in a white dress shirt, me and Marisol in similar black dresses.

I guess Alistair and I went to the dance after all. Just not as a couple.

I don't touch the joker cards on my wall. I don't care what Karen says—I'm not going to take them down.

I load everything else into a couple of boxes and shove them in my closet.

Later that evening, I'm slumped over my laptop at the kitchen table, searching the internet for the palm reader. Finding her is proving tougher than I expected. I sent an email to the generic email address on the night-market website the other day to ask if they had any information about her, but I haven't had a response yet.

I think for a minute, then I do a search for the night market plus the word *crystals*. A second later, an old newspaper article pops up. Apparently, our town held a psychic fair back in 2011. I zoom in on the picture that accompanies the article: a woman wearing a flowing caftan, an orange butterfly clipped in her long, wavy white hair, staring into a crystal ball.

I sit up straighter. It's her! It's my palm reader!

Unfortunately, there's no mention of her name in the caption or in the article. There is a sponsor listed, however—Crystal Dreams. A quick Google search tells me that it's a shop located in the next town. I could just send them an email, but I decide that it might be better to go into the shop. That way, if they don't know my palm reader, maybe they'll still be able to help me get another magical crystal.

Dad wanders into the kitchen. His hair is messy, as if he's been running his fingers through it. He's still in his paint clothes—he was touching up a few spots in the bathroom that we missed. He's been so busy that we skipped dinner.

"You want to go grab a pizza?" Dad asks as Napoleon scratches at the back door to be let back inside. He opens the door and Napoleon bounds over to me, his nails scrabbling against the wood floor, and nudges me with his nose. "You could use the practice driving at night."

I grimace. I've been avoiding getting behind the wheel since the day he let me drive to Castle Hardware. Still, I guess the only way to learn is by doing. It's late enough that maybe there won't be that many cars on the road, and Pizza Kitchen is only a few blocks away. Besides, it's not like I can do anything else to track down the palm reader tonight.

"Sure." I close my laptop. "Pizza sounds good."

Driving is a little easier tonight, although I'm still super tense.

"Em, you don't have to clutch the wheel so hard," Dad says as I pull onto the street. "Just relax."

But it's not that easy.

The traffic light in front of me turns yellow and I hit the brake.

"Yellow means slow down, not stop," Dad says. "You still had time to go through the intersection."

"You're making me nervous!"

He sighs.

There are a bunch of cars in the Pizza Kitchen parking lot. We go inside the restaurant and settle into a red-leather booth. I'm studying the sticky laminated menu when the waiter arrives.

"Welcome to Pizza Kitchen," a voice says. "Oh, hey, Emelia."

I glance up, my breath catching in my throat.

Ben.

"You work here?" I ask him.

He gives me that lazy grin that still has an effect on me, even if I wish it wouldn't. When he smiles at me like that, I think about how we once were, back at the beginning. Back when I believed I'd made the right choice.

"You sound surprised," he says.

I am surprised. The Ben I knew was work-averse. Getting a job—especially one that involved waiting on people—was not something he ever expressed interest in.

Then again, maybe the Ben in this life is different. Maybe he's a better person. It's weird to know so many things about him, to have so many memories of the two of us together, when he doesn't remember any of it.

I chew my lip. Maybe there is something worse than breaking up with someone—having them forget you, and what you once meant to each other, altogether. As much as I was done with him at the end, there was a time when he was all I could think about. All I wanted. At the sight of him, those feelings start to resurface. I'm not as relieved as I should be that we're not together anymore.

"What can I get you?" Ben is waiting, pen poised above his

notepad. His blond hair is slicked back instead of its usual rumpled mess.

"What do you think, Em—you want to split a medium pepperoni?" Dad asks me.

"Yeah, okay." Although, truthfully, I don't feel all that hungry anymore. Running into Ben again has thrown me.

Dad orders us a couple of root beers and Ben writes it all down on his notepad, then collects our menus and disappears through the swinging doors into the kitchen.

"You know him?" Dad asks.

Yes, and you do too. Or you did, before I went and changed everything.

My dad liked Ben, even if my mom wasn't crazy about him. They used to talk about cars and football, two subjects that bored my mom and me to tears.

I swallow past the lump in my throat. "We go to school together."

Dad nodded.

I wonder what will happen when I find the palm reader and change my past again—if Ben will still be with Olivia, if he'll still be working here. If maybe, in the next version of my life, we'll be friends.

I feel guilty that by changing my life, I'm messing with others. If I'm able to change everything again, then I should probably just put it all back the way it was—but then that will mean missing out on my chance with Alistair.

And I just can't give up on the idea of us.

CHAPTER
15

I arrive at Castle Hardware the next morning half an hour before the store opens. My shift is supposed to start in five minutes—apparently, I'll be helping prep the store for opening, whatever that entails—but the front door is locked. I peer through the glass. The lights are on, but I don't see anyone.

Great. How am I supposed to get inside?

I've been working here for months, so this is definitely something that I'm supposed to know. If anyone catches me out here, looking confused, there are going to be questions. Questions that I have no idea how to answer.

Just when I'm about to panic—only two more minutes until my shift starts—another car pulls into the lot. The passenger door of a blue Prius opens and Avery climbs out. She says something to the driver, then closes the door and gives me a sunny smile.

"Hey, Emelia," she says, sliding her mini backpack over her

shoulder as the Prius drives away. She's wearing jean cutoffs and her Castle Hardware vest is covered in a lot of the same buttons as Violet's. It's clearly something they did together like me and Alistair and our joker cards, and I wonder what it means that she hasn't removed hers. Maybe it doesn't mean anything. Or maybe it means everything.

"Hi. I thought you weren't working today?" I ask.

Avery yawns. "Angela called in sick, so Mike asked if I could fill in for her. I decided I needed the money more than I need to avoid Violet," she says. "Although I was out way too late last night, so I probably should have chosen sleep instead."

I'm pretty sure Violet has no idea about this last-minute shift change. She's blithely doing whatever it is she does to help open the store, about to be blindsided by Avery showing up when she's not expecting her. And what's worse than running into an ex when you're not prepared to see them?

Nothing. That's what.

Avery starts to walk around to the back of the building. I follow behind her, taking out my phone to shoot Violet a quick heads-up text. A last-minute warning that she's about to come face-to-face with Avery is better than nothing.

Avery stops in front of the rolled-up steel door used for receiving deliveries and pushes the buzzer mounted on the wall. A few seconds later, the door clicks open. A man with a long gray beard is standing on the other side of the door, holding a clipboard.

"Hi, Charlie," Avery says.

He grunts in response. Avery signs the clipboard, so I sign it too, and we scoot past him.

"Guess I'm not the only one who needs a little more sleep," she whispers as we walk through the back warehouse and into the store.

I continue to stick close to her because I have no idea where I'm going or what I'm supposed to be doing. I stumbled through my last shift, but I'm not sure how much longer I'm going to get away with not knowing how to do this job.

Violet's in the paint section, standing beside a metal cart stacked with cardboard boxes. She slices open the top of one of the boxes with a utility knife and pulls out a package of paint rollers.

She glances over at Avery and me and her eyes widen. So, I guess she didn't get my message.

"Hi, Violet," Avery says.

Violet clears her face of all emotion. She nods and then busies herself by threading the package of paint rollers onto a metal display hook, her hands shaking slightly.

"I like your hair."

Violet's newly dyed ice-blond hair hangs in choppy waves halfway down her back.

She shrugs. "I thought I could use a change."

"Well, it looks great," Avery says, her voice full of false cheer.

God, this is so awkward. These are two people who spent almost a year together—who loved each other—and their breakup has reduced them to small talk. Still, I guess it's better than no talk.

Violet's cheeks start to slowly burn. She may look like an ice queen, but she's beginning to melt, and I know that she doesn't want either of us around for that.

"Okay, well, we should probably clock in," I say. "See you later, Vi."

It turns out that Avery is in the sports department today while I work the front counter, so she is of no help to me. For the next twenty minutes I stand in front of my till, trying to look like I know what I'm doing. Just before nine, Mike, the manager, comes up to open the front door. A ring of keys hangs from the belt loop on his jeans, jingling with each step he takes. Those keys are an early warning system—he's like a cat with a bell on his collar. There's no way he can sneak up on anyone, which is a very good thing for me.

As a few customers trickle into the store—a small wave of early risers and do-it-yourselfers—Violet slips behind the front counter to join me. Her eyes meet mine just long enough for me to tell she's been crying, before they skip away.

"Sorry I was such a freak earlier," she says. "I just didn't know what to do. It's the first time I've seen Avery since she dumped me."

"The first time is always the worst."

It makes me think of Ben. Running into him at the night market and the pizza place was weird, and we didn't even break up. He doesn't remember our relationship, so there's not anything for me to feel awkward about, and it still sucked. I can't imagine having to work with him.

Violet sighs. "I don't think it's going to get any better. I'm never going to be able to talk to her. This is the worst." She punches her password into her register to unlock it, her fingers stabbing angrily at the keys. I notice her bracelet, small gold nuts laid out in a geometric pattern and held together by a thin gold wire.

"That's beautiful. Did you make it?"

She nods.

I'm amazed at how she can turn something so plain into something so pretty.

Violet takes it off and hands it to me. "You can have it. I'll make another one."

"Are you sure?" I put the bracelet on, admiring how it looks on my wrist, just as the front doors open and Alistair walks into the store.

My heart catches. I don't know how it's possible, but I swear, every time I see him, he just gets hotter. His wild black curls poke out from under a gray beanie and he's carrying two iced coffees.

"What are you doing here?" Violet says to him. "You're not on the schedule today."

"And good morning to you, too." He sets the coffees on the counter and slides them toward me and Violet. "I knew you were both working, so I figured it was a good time to talk to you about my documentary."

"What documentary?"

Alistair's eyes narrow. "Wait. You changed your hair."

"What documentary?" she repeats.

"I'm going to film the Catan competition as part of my application to USC."

Violet picks up her coffee. "And this involves us how?"

"Welllll . . . I'd like you to star in it."

She snorts. "I don't think so."

"Oh, come on, Vi," he says. "Please? I need you. Em's already agreed to do it."

Violet frowns and glares at me. "You didn't mention this."

"I forgot," I say. I didn't forget, really. I just figured that since it was Alistair's project, he should be the one to ask her.

Alistair steps out of the way as a woman walks up with a bicycle pump. Violet quickly rings her through, then turns back to him.

"What is it that I have to do?" she asks.

Alistair smiles. "Just play in the competition. And be yourself."

"It would be better if I could be someone else."

"Why would you want to be anyone else?" He reaches forward and gently tweaks her nose. "You're perfect, just the way you are."

Violet swats his hand away, but I can tell she's trying not to laugh. "Fine. I'll do it."

"Thank you."

Alistair stares at her, a weird smile on his face.

Violet narrows her eyes. "Why are you smiling at me like that?"

"Uh . . . okay. I actually had another ulterior motive for showing up this morning." He scratches his ear. "I've been thinking about your grand gesture."

Violet whips around and glares at me. "You told him?"

"I didn't know it was a secret," I say, fiddling with my new bracelet. "And I thought he'd have some good ideas."

"Yeah, well, thanks, but I don't," Alistair says. "I do, however, have some friendly advice: Don't do it."

Violet huffs out a breath and crosses her arms. Alistair should know by now that if you tell Violet that she can't do something, it pretty much guarantees that she will want to do it. "Why not?"

"Just trust me. I'm telling you this as a friend. It's not a good idea."

The sound of keys jingling keeps Violet from responding. We straighten, frantically looking for something that will help us appear busy, as Mike walks up.

"Alistair," he says. "Why are you here?"

"I just had to stop by to grab some cat litter," Alistair says.

Mike scans the counter. "I don't see any cat litter, but I do see coffee cups," he says. "Coffee is for breaks, ladies. Are you on a break right now?"

Violet and I shake our heads. I grab our cups and place them beneath the counter.

"Mr. Stewart, if you're so eager to be here, I can find something for you to do," he adds.

"Talk to you guys later," Alistair says. He salutes Mike and then takes off.

Mike hangs around the front for a few more minutes, probably to make sure that Alistair doesn't come back, before the walkie-talkie attached to his belt crackles and a voice asks him to come to kitchenware.

"Maybe Alistair is right," Violet says, once he's gone. "Maybe trying to win Avery back is a bad idea."

"I don't think so. If you don't try, you're never going to know."

I know a little something about living with regret. Not taking a chance on Alistair was one of the worst mistakes I'd ever made. I've really messed things up, and I don't want Violet to have to spend the rest of her life wondering what could have happened if she'd just made a different choice.

"I need to do this," she says. "Besides, I already thought of a really cool grand gesture. Avery always complained that I never planned anything. What if I sent her on a scavenger hunt to all the places we used to go when we were together. And then, at the end, she finds me at the park, waiting for her with a picnic."

"That sounds pretty complicated."

"That's the whole point of a grand gesture! It's supposed to be complicated. You have to put the effort in," she says. "And a picnic is definitely putting the effort in. Especially because I hate picnics."

"Okay, but how are you going to get her to agree to do the scavenger hunt?"

Violet frowns. "Well, I haven't worked out all the kinks yet."

A rush of customers starts to line up at the counter, putting an end to our conversation. And by the time we've rung everyone through, it's time for Violet's break. I don't see her again for the rest of my shift.

16

It takes me forty-five minutes and two bus transfers to get to Crystal Dreams. The nondescript little shop is in a strip mall, wedged between a sandwich shop and a nail salon.

A bell above the door jingles as I walk inside. The store has a woodsy, almost smoky smell. Pan-flute music plays over the speakers.

A man glances up from behind the counter, where he's perched on a stool reading a book. He has curly gray hair, and he's wearing John Lennon glasses, as well as a huge teardrop-shaped purple crystal around his neck.

"Welcome," he says, closing his book. "Just browsing, or can I help you find something?"

"Actually, I'm hoping you can help me find some*one*." I pull out my phone and show him the photo of the palm reader from the newspaper article.

He squints at the picture. "Sure, that's Irene," he says.

A fissure of excitement goes through me. "Do you know how I can reach her?"

He shakes his head. "It's been a few years since I've run into her."

"Do you know her last name?" If I have her last name, then I have a better chance of tracking her down on the internet.

"Sorry, I don't."

Well, that sucks.

I take my crystal out of my pocket and set it down on the counter in front of him. "Do you have anything similar to this?"

"Rutilated quartz," he says. "I don't have any right now, unfortunately."

"Do you know anything about it's, um, special properties?" None of the research I've done on this crystal has turned up anything about its ability to change the past. I'm beginning to worry that it must somehow be unique to this particular rock.

"Well, it can certainly cleanse and recharge your chakras," he says. "Which I think is pretty darned special."

I frown. It's clear that he doesn't know anything about what this crystal can actually do, which just reaffirms that I need to find the palm reader.

"So, you have no idea where I might find Irene?"

He thinks. "I did hear that she had a shop somewhere. Maybe try down around Park and Sixth."

Great. That intersection is in a super shady part of town, not a place that I want to go alone, even in the daylight. I debate whether I should go there now anyway, but it's all the way across town and I'm supposed to meet my friends at Bonus Round shortly.

"Okay, thanks."

"Good luck," he says.

✳ ✳ ✳

Bonus Round is packed when I arrive there an hour later. Violet's already set up our game board and is quietly studying players at other tables while eating a giant chocolate chip cookie.

I plunk down in the leather chair across from her.

"I think you're right about the scavenger hunt," she says, picking up the thread of our earlier conversation about her plans to win Avery back. "It's too complicated. I know I said it's supposed to be, but I haven't been able to figure out how I'd get her to do it. And picnics are overrated anyway. Avery's supposed to love me again just because I packed her a sandwich?" She shakes her head.

"So, what are you going to do instead?"

"That's the problem. I don't know."

The door opens and Alistair and Marisol walk in. I'm surprised that he convinced her to come—getting her out has been nearly impossible lately. I know she's busy with her embroidery, too busy to even answer my texts.

Alistair spots me and smiles, sending my pulse into overdrive. He's about to head over to our table when Marisol grabs his arm and pulls him back. Her eyes briefly meet mine before skipping away. My stomach sinks.

Without glancing in our direction again, Marisol marches him down the corridor that leads to the washrooms.

"What's that all about?" Violet says.

"I don't know."

But that's not true—I think I do know. As careful as I've been to hide my feelings for Alistair, maybe I haven't been careful enough. Maybe Marisol has figured out that I have a thing for her boyfriend and she's realized that I'm the worst kind of friend. It would definitely explain why she's been avoiding me.

I should probably leave well enough alone, but I feel like I need to clear the air with her. I want her to know how important she is to me. I know Marisol doesn't remember how I treated her when I was with Ben, but I'll never forget. I can never make it up to her, but I still have to try.

If she confronts me about my feelings for Alistair, I don't know what I'm going to say. I guess anything but the truth will work.

"Em, where are you going?" Violet says as I stand up and follow them.

I weave through the tables until I reach the corridor. I peek around the corner. Marisol's back is to me. Alistair is leaning against the wall, his arms crossed. I shouldn't eavesdrop on their conversation—it's wrong—but I want to know what I'm about to walk into.

"—didn't tell me she was going to be here. It's so awkward," Marisol says.

"This is ridiculous. You have to face her sometime."

"You should have told me she was here!"

"You wouldn't have come if I'd told you."

My stomach plummets. I was right—she's avoiding me.

"Exactly. You're trying to push me into . . ." The hiss of the espresso machine behind me cuts off the rest of Marisol's sentence.

"You're not being fair—" Alistair says.

"Al, you promised!"

"Yeah, okay, I did . . . but how much longer are you going to hold me to this? I can't keep this up forev—" He stops as his eyes meet mine over Marisol's shoulder.

Marisol whips around. Her eyes burn into me and I realize coming after them was a mistake. Not everything is my business. It's not Emelia-Alistair-and-Marisol anymore. It's the two of them and me.

My cheeks flush. "Uh, I just wanted to check to make sure that you guys are all right."

"We're fine," Marisol says tightly. She turns back around, dismissing me.

Feeling humiliated, I head back to the table.

"They're fighting," I tell Violet as I sit back down in my chair.

"Yeah, that was pretty obvious," she says. "Now, fill me in. What are they fighting about?"

I shrug. "I'm not sure. It was too loud to really hear."

I'm too ashamed to tell her the truth, even though I know Violet wouldn't judge me. And it's not like it would be a surprise—she already suspects that I have more-than-friends feelings for Alistair. I just don't know how to tell her what I overheard without bursting into tears.

Violet cocks an eyebrow at me, but she lets it go. She breaks off a piece of her cookie and hands it to me. I don't feel much like eating, but I take a bite anyway. Chewing will prevent me from having to talk.

A minute later, Alistair walks over and drops into the chair beside me.

"Where's Marisol?" Violet asks him.

"She went home."

Her eyes widen. "So, what? She just took one look at us and left? What did she do, slip out the back door?"

"It's not personal," he replies, but his gaze flicks to me. "I sort of sprung you guys on her. She's anxious about getting her orders done and she's just really overwhelmed and stressed out right now. She's not acting like herself."

He's lying to spare my feelings. The truth is, Marisol doesn't want to be around me because she knows that I'm hot for her boyfriend. And I'm pretty sure her boyfriend knows it too.

The cookie is sticking in my throat.

"And she didn't care that you're staying here with us?" Violet asks.

Alistair frowns. "We don't have to spend every minute together."

"That doesn't answer my question, but I get it—none of my business."

He picks up a road game piece and fiddles with it. "If you

must know, I told her I had to stay behind to talk to you about the documentary." He sets the white road down on the board, between two hexes, forest and pasture. "I have an idea for your big grand gesture."

Violet perks up.

"I thought you were against her trying to win Avery back," I say.

Alistair glances at me. "I changed my mind," he says. "I'm not convinced it's going to do any good, but Vi, if you still want to do something, I'll help you."

"I still want to do something," she says. "What's your idea?"

He puts a settlement down beside his road, then gestures for me to take my turn. "I think you should pull a Lloyd Dobler."

Violet's forehead wrinkles. "What the heck is a Lloyd Dobler?"

"*Say Anything.*" I place my red road and settlement on the lumber hex on the other side of the board. "You know, that movie where the guy stands below the girl's window with a boom box."

"You want me to stand under Avery's window with a boom box?" Violet asks him.

"Sort of," Alistair says. "But I think you should actually sing to her."

Violet snorts. "Uh, there's only one problem with that scenario: I can't sing."

"You can too," he says. "I was in junior choir with you, remember?"

"*Everyone* was in junior choir, whether they could sing or

not. And I cannot sing. You would know that if you'd stood any-where near me."

"Look, do you want Avery back or not?" Alistair says.

Violet nods.

"Then, in your own words, you need a grand gesture. And what's grander than a serenade?"

Violet considers this. "But what would I even sing?"

"What's her favorite song?" I ask.

"I don't know, she has a bunch. I guess I could do something by Ariana Grande," she says. "Ooh, maybe I could put my hair up in her signature ponytail?" She gathers her blond hair on top of her head.

"Whatever works, I guess," Alistair says.

I lean back in my chair. "Where are you going to do this?"

"Good question. I can't do it at her house—Avery would kill me if I did anything in front of her parents."

"You could do it at work," Alistair suggests.

"You want her to sing to Avery at Castle Hardware?" I ask him.

"Think about it: Avery will be working, so she can't just leave. She's a captive audience. She'll have to listen to you."

Violet slowly nods. "It's worth a try, I guess."

I'm impressed with the lengths that she's going to in order to try to win Avery back—I just hope that Avery is impressed too.

✳ CHAPTER ✳
17

I loosen my grip on Violet's waist as she steers her scooter up to the curb in front of an abandoned building. The brick storefront is covered in graffiti and papered with flyers, garbage blowing along the street like tumbleweeds. I unwind my arms from around her waist and climb off the back of her scooter.

"Are you sure this is where the palm reader is supposed to be?" she asks me.

"Yes," I answer, taking off my helmet and running a hand through my hair. I haven't told Violet much, just that I'm looking for a palm reader who once gave me a very accurate reading, and I wanted to see her again. Coming to this super sketchy area by myself didn't seem like the best idea, so I asked her to come with me.

I've tried searching for Irene again online, but I've still had no luck unearthing her. The only clue I have, besides her first name, is from the man at Crystal Dreams who mentioned that she might be in this area.

"I don't remember where her shop is, exactly," I say, my cheeks reddening from the lie. "But it's somewhere around here."

Violet makes us carry our helmets, rather than stow them under the seat like we usually do. She casts an uncertain look back at her scooter as we start to walk down the block, past a money-loan place and a pawn shop with bars on its windows. The sun is out in full force this afternoon, beating down on us.

"Do you really believe that someone can tell your future just by reading the lines on your palm?" she asks.

I shrug. The palm reader never actually read my palm, so I can't say. But obviously she possesses some kind of magic.

Violet steps around a broken beer bottle. "What is it that you want to know, anyway?"

"I just thought it would be fun."

Violet chews her lip. "Maybe I should ask her if she sees Avery and me getting back together." She wrinkles her nose. "On second thought, I'm not sure I want to hear the answer to that. What if she tells me that we'll never be together again? I don't think I could take it."

We reach the end of the block.

"Are you certain this is the right neighborhood?" Violet asks me again. We're stopped in front of an empty storefront, a FOR LEASE sign posted in the window.

I nod. The guy in Crystal Dreams definitely said Park and Sixth. I'm about to give up and suggest we get out of here when

I spot a playing card on the ground, right in front of the empty store.

My heart starts to race. I know what it's going to be before I even turn it over. I bend down and pick it up and, sure enough, it's a joker. The same black-and-white joker card that I picked up at the night market, right before I noticed the palm reader's tent.

"Hey, Em, look at this," Violet says. She points to an unlit neon sign of an open hand in the window, right beside the FOR LEASE sign.

My mouth goes dry. This is it. This is Irene's place!

"It doesn't look like anyone has been here in a while," she adds as I slip the card into my pocket. There's a bunch of newspapers and junk mail piled in front of the door. The windows are filthy, making it hard to see inside.

My shoulders slump. She's not here. This is a dead end.

"Maybe she moved somewhere else," Violet says. "Somewhere a little less scary."

Maybe. But I have no idea where else to look.

Violet grabs one of the pieces of junk mail off the stoop. "Irene Kowalski," she says, flipping the yellow envelope over to show me the name on the front. "Is that her?"

I smile and take the envelope from her. "That's her!"

I pull out my phone and google her name. She pops up right away as the contact for a shop called the Mystic Moon. The website is under construction—all that's on it is the shop's address. We're standing in front of the address to that empty shop, so it doesn't seem like she's relocated somewhere else yet.

There's a phone number at the bottom of the page. I can't exactly call her, especially when Violet's staring at me, so I decide to do it later, once I get home.

"I bet there are a million other palm readers around," Violet says. "Do you want to try someone else?"

I shake my head. "It has to be her."

To her credit, Violet doesn't ask me why. We just walk back to her scooter and wind back through the city streets. We're on our way to Alistair's so he can help her practice for her grand gesture at Castle Hardware, but all I can think about is finding a moment to be alone so I can call the palm reader and finally get my life back on track.

18

Violet wasn't kidding—she really can't sing. I have second-hand embarrassment just watching her.

I've been listening to her butcher Ariana Grande for the past half hour. She's out of tune and totally out of step with the music, racing through the song faster than the notes can keep up with her.

"Okay, so you're still a little off-key and you're a little shouty," Alistair says when she finishes the song. "Let's try it again."

Violet's mouth pinches and she crosses her arms. "This isn't going to work."

"Don't give up, we're going to get there." He nods at me to start the music. I'm sitting in a lawn chair by the garage door, playing DJ on his phone.

"'I'm so into you, I can barely breathe,'" Violet starts. She sings, her back stiff, not looking at either of us. She's taken

Alistair's advice and lowered her voice, but she still sounds pretty bad.

I smile encouragingly at her, trying not to wince as she slaughters the song.

Violet finishes, the music trailing behind her. She looks at me hopefully. "Any better?"

"Much better." But I can feel my cheeks turning red.

Her face falls. "You're a terrible liar, Em," she says. "Ugh, this is a bad idea. I told you guys I suck!"

Alistair walks over and hands her a glass of water. "You don't suck. You just need a bit more practice."

"Like a thousand years more practice," she mumbles, taking a drink.

"You're rushing through the song. You're not trying to be the first person to the finish line; you want to take your time. Put some emotion into it," he says. "Slow down and really feel the lyrics. Here, I'll show you."

Alistair gestures for me to restart the music. Four beats of percussion and then he starts to sing. "'I'm so into you, I can barely breathe.'"

He doesn't have a rock-star voice, but it is strong and clear . . . and hearing him sing is incredibly hot. His gray eyes lock on mine, pinning me to my chair. I should look away from him, but I can't. Every note out of his mouth vibrates through me, a promise of what we could be, if we were alone—and he didn't already have a girlfriend.

"'And all I want to do is to fall in deep . . .'"

A slow smile spreads across his face. Violet has faded into

the background, and it's just the two of us. It's like he's singing directly to me.

Stop it, I tell myself. Alistair's not singing *to* me; he's just showing Violet how he thinks she should perform the song, all sexy and stuff. It doesn't mean anything. It can't mean anything, because he is with someone else. My best friend.

This is probably all in my imagination anyway. Alistair hasn't really given me any indication that he still feels the way he did the night he showed up at my house. He's only giving Violet some friendly direction.

Still, my heart can't help responding—it's beating a mile a minute. The temperature seems to have gone up several degrees, and I've broken out in a sweat.

When he finishes the song, his eyes shift away from me and the spell is broken. Alistair clears his throat. "So, uh, maybe more like that."

Violet tries again—and again and again and again. Her performance never gets anywhere near Alistair's level, but she does manage to pack a bit more passion into it. She's loosened up a little and she no longer looks like she's being forced to sing against her will.

"I think that's about as good as it's going to get." She tugs on one of the dangly earrings she fashioned from a screw and some thin copper wire. "Are you guys sure that I should go through with this?"

Alistair nods. "Remember, it's not all about how you sound . . . it's the feeling behind it." His eyes skip to me, then away again.

"Okay, well, I guess I'm really going to do this, then," she says. "Avery's on the schedule on Thursday—and before either of you ask, yes, I check her schedule." She slides her hands into the back pockets of her black cargo shorts. "The sooner I do this, the sooner we'll be back together and I can pretend that our breakup was all just a bad dream."

She might not have to worry about that for much longer. If I can get ahold of the palm reader and get another crystal, then, with any luck, she and Avery won't ever have broken up.

"Thursday's perfect," Alistair says. "I'm working too."

Violet pokes me in the shoulder. "Em, I know you're not on the schedule, but will you come in anyway?"

"Of course."

She glances at her phone. "We should probably get going. I need to get up at insanely early o'clock. Stupid morning shifts."

Alistair holds out a hand to help me out of the chair. The feel of his fingers in mine makes my heart take off again. He pulls me to my feet. He gives my hand a quick squeeze before letting go.

I think about that squeeze all the way home.

And the minute Violet drops me off, I pull out my phone to call the palm reader. It's late, but I'm hoping that I can leave a message. I stand by my front door, under the porch light, and dial the number listed on the Mystic Moon website. The call goes through, but an automated voice says the number isn't in service.

My shoulders slump.

Great. How am I going to find her now?

CHAPTER
19

Marisol tosses the skein of embroidery floss back onto the shelf at the craft store. "It's too pink," she says, sighing wearily. "It needs to be lighter—like the color of ballet shoes."

I survey the thread display in front of us. There are approximately eight million different shades of pink—the one that she requires for her project has to be here. I pick up a skein several hues lighter than the one she just rejected and show it to her.

She shakes her head and pushes a lock of her unruly hair out of her eyes. She looks exhausted, like she hasn't slept in days. Marisol's not exactly a stranger to pushing herself—her grade-point average has never dipped below a 4.0, and she takes part in a ton of extracurriculars during the school year—but this is summer. The only thing she should be worrying about is making sure she's wearing a high enough SPF.

I've never seen her this stressed out. I'm genuinely beginning to worry about her.

"You really should take a break." I wince as soon as the words are out of my mouth, because telling her to take a break is not only super unhelpful but will probably also make her super mad.

Sure enough, her expression darkens. "I'm fine," she snaps.

Yes. You seem totally fine, I think.

She pushes her glasses up onto her forehead and rubs her eyes. "Sorry," she mumbles. "I'm not mad at you; I've just got a lot on my mind right now."

I squeeze her arm. "Do you want to talk about it?" Clearly something is weighing on her. Something that must go beyond taking on too many embroidery projects.

Her face softens. For a moment, I think that she might open up and tell me what's bothering her—the old Marisol told me everything about her life, and vice versa—but all she says is, "It's nothing. I just had a fight with someone. But I'm the worst for taking it out on you. Sorry again."

I chew my bottom lip. I wonder if the person she fought with is Alistair. Maybe they're having problems and she doesn't want to involve me because I'm friends with both of them.

What if they break up?

I feel a burst of hope in my chest, quickly followed by shame. Marisol's not the worst—I am. I'm a terrible friend. I'm scheming on how to get my hands on another crystal so that I can rewrite history and make sure that Alistair ends up my boyfriend instead of hers. And while I can tell myself that it's okay because the two of them aren't destined to be together, that I'm just putting things right and he's actually meant for me, the truth of it is that I'll be taking something away from her. Even if she won't remember being his girlfriend, I will always remember how much I suck.

Maybe I should just leave everything as is. Maybe this reality is exactly what I deserve.

"Now, please distract me with tales from your life," Marisol says, grabbing a handful of lime-green floss from the shelf and dropping it into the plastic basket at her feet, which is already filled with needles and fabric. "Tell me what's going on with you."

I shrug. "Nothing exciting."

Talking about my life is tricky because I don't know what we've already discussed. Like, have I broken the news to her that my parents are getting divorced and that our house is for sale, or have I kept that to myself?

"Come on, Em," she says. "What happened to that lifeguard you couldn't shut up about earlier this summer?"

I stare at her, frozen in panic. I have no idea who she's talking about. I don't know any lifeguards . . .

My scalp prickles. It's disturbing that I don't know details about my own life, especially when it comes to something as monumental as who I've been into. It makes me question whether I was even upset about Alistair and Marisol coupling up. Maybe I didn't care. Maybe I was happy for them.

This is all so unsettling.

Fortunately, I'm saved from having to give her the name of my lifeguard crush by the sound of our phones, which buzz at the exact same time. Alistair's sent a group text, checking in to see what time we'll be back at Marisol's house. We're all supposed to watch a movie together.

I watch Marisol closely, to see how she reacts to him texting her, but her expression doesn't change. So I don't think he's the person she's upset with. My heart shrinks a little. If I were a better person, I'd be happy that she isn't fighting with her boyfriend.

Maybe she had it out with her parents, I think. Although I don't know why she'd be secretive about arguing with them.

"Rob," she says.

Huh?

"Rob Felton, your hot lifeguard."

Wait, I had a crush on Rob Felton, the guy my parents pay to cut our lawn?

I mean, Rob's good-looking in a frat-boy sort of way, so I guess I can see it, at least on a surface level. But I've never had an actual conversation with him—that I'm aware of, at least.

"Oh, him," I say. "I'm over it."

But Marisol's only half listening to me. She's distracted by some pink floss that she deems close enough for her needs. She adds it to her pile and we head to the checkout.

* * *

"Stop trying to make *Mean Girls* happen," Alistair says an hour later. The three of us are in Marisol's basement, standing in front of her parents' DVD collection, trying to agree on a movie.

"But it's my favorite," Marisol says. "And I've had a really bad day."

Alistair nods thoughtfully. "I knew it. I sensed a disturbance in the Force earlier," he says. "All right, I give in—on the condition that we watch *Weekend at Bernie's* directly afterward."

Marisol nods. "Deal."

"Hello?" I interject. "Don't I get a say in this?"

"Two against one, O'Malley." Alistair drapes an arm around my shoulders. His fingers graze my bare arm and my entire body starts to buzz. "You know the rules."

"Well, I want to renegotiate."

"Two. Against. One," he repeats. He still has his arm around me. It's very hard to think clearly when he's this close to me.

"I renege on the deal," Marisol says, twisting her dark hair into a topknot. "I didn't think it through. Em would have sided with me anyway." She walks over and plunks down on the couch.

I smile at Alistair. "Two against one, Stewart."

"Ugh, fine," he replies. "What are your terms?"

"Anything other than *Weekend at Bernie's*."

He rolls his eyes. "How did I know you were going to say that?"

"You must have ESPN," I say, pulling out a *Mean Girls* quote of my own.

He catches the reference and grins. "You drive a hard bargain. How about *Austin Powers*, then?"

"Yeah, baby," I say.

He laughs.

Marisol sighs and roots through the bag of supplies we picked up at the craft store. "Have I ever told you that you guys are weird?"

"Plenty of times," Alistair says.

I duck out from underneath his arm and head over to the couch. Alistair puts the movie on. Instead of claiming the beanbag chair or taking the spot beside Marisol—who's already picked up her embroidery hoop—he settles in beside me, leaving a large gap between me and Marisol at the other end of the couch.

He rests his arm along the back of the couch. I watch him out of the corner of my eye. What is he doing?

As soon as the movie starts, the doorbell rings.

"That'll be the pizza guy," Marisol says, setting her embroidery hoop on the coffee table.

Alistair pops up. "I've got it." He reaches into the back pocket of his jeans and pulls out his grandfather's old black leather wallet. His fingers are shaking and he fumbles and drops his wallet.

"Crap," he says as money, receipts, and a joker card slip to the floor.

A warm feeling spreads through me. I can't believe he still has this card. I found it years ago in the park. I thought about keeping it for myself—it was special, with a glittery gold background—but ultimately, I decided to give Alistair the card. I'm still not even sure why.

And there's something else. The strip of photo-booth pictures of the two of us from the night we went to get gelato.

It's not a big deal, I tell myself. He probably just shoved it in his wallet when I gave it to him and never thought about it again. It doesn't mean anything.

But when I sneak a look at him, I see that the tips of his ears are glowing red. Alistair kneels and starts frantically gathering everything up into a messy pile.

So maybe it is a big deal. Maybe I'm not the only one still having these feelings after all.

I glance at Marisol. She's bent over her embroidery hoop, trying to unpick a stitch. I don't think that she saw the photos. My shoulders relax. My best friend discovering that I have feelings for her boyfriend—and that her boyfriend might possibly have feelings for me—is my worst-case scenario. I've hurt Marisol enough in the past, even if she doesn't remember it, and I never want to do that again. The only way Alistair and I will ever be together is if I find another crystal.

The doorbell rings again and he stands. He disappears up the stairs, taking them two at a time. I hear him open the door and the muted sound of his voice as he talks to the pizza guy. The door closes, and a minute later he bounds back down the stairs.

"Pierogi pizza," Alistair says brightly, setting the box in the middle of the coffee table, along with the plates he must have grabbed from the kitchen. This time he chooses the beanbag chair instead of the couch. He turns on the movie and neither of us looks at the other for the rest of the night.

✳ CHAPTER ✳
20

The next morning, Violet wipes her palms on her Castle Hardware vest, her face pale. She's behind the customer-service desk, her blond hair pulled back into Ariana Grande's trademark high ponytail.

"Are you sure you want to go through with this?" I ask as she shrugs out of her vest. Underneath, she's wearing a tight white lace dress that falls just above her knee, leaving only a thin strip of bare skin visible before her legs disappear into tall gray suede boots. I have no idea how she managed to slip past Mike, the manager, in this video-vixen getup.

"Nope," she says. "But I'm going to do it anyway. I just hope I don't make a complete fool of myself."

"You're not going to make a fool of yourself," Alistair reassures her. He's behind the counter with her, his dark hair all just-rolled-out-of-bed sexy. His eyes meet mine and then quickly skip away, like he hasn't quite gotten past what happened at Marisol's last night. "You're going to be great, Vi."

Violet lets out a puff of air and rolls her shoulders to release the tension. "Okay," she says, shaking out her arms. "Let's get this over with."

Alistair holds out his hand and helps guide her up the step stool and onto the wood counter. She sways on the heels of her sky-high boots, like she's standing on the deck of a ship in the middle of a violent storm.

"Please, please, do not fall," Alistair says.

"Who cares about falling? I'm worried that everyone will see up my dress," she replies, tugging the hem down.

I shake my head. "You're fine."

A woman with a red plastic basket looped over her arm glances curiously at Violet as she walks past us. The store only just opened, so there aren't too many customers yet.

Alistair passes Violet the intercom, which is really just a phone connected to a bunch of speakers that are set into the ceiling all around the store. She takes a deep breath as she holds the handset up to her mouth. The speakers above us crackle.

"Avery Macdonald . . . this one's for you," she says.

Alistair hits play on his cell phone, and his long arm shoots into the air so the intercom can pick up the music. The opening thumping notes of "Into You" float through the store.

"'I'm so into you, I can barely breathe,'" Violet sings, and I relax a little. Maybe it's the distortion from the speakers, but her voice actually doesn't sound half-bad. As people start to figure out what's happening, they drift toward us, and pretty soon a small crowd of customers and staff has gathered in front of the customer-service desk, staring up at the unexpected sight of a girl performing an impromptu concert in a hardware store. Violet's feet are planted as if they're encased in blocks of cement, but the rest of her body sways.

Mike pushes his way through the crowd. "What on earth is going on here?" he yells. "Violet, get down from there right now!"

Violet looks past him, scanning the crowd for Avery. I shoot a panicked glance at Alistair, but he's busy fiddling with the intercom. The volume suddenly ratchets up and drowns Mike out. We probably should have thought about how to deal with his reaction to Violet's grand gesture.

Mike huffs. He takes a step forward, like he's about to slip behind the counter and yank Violet off the counter, but I grab his arm. I can't let him stop her—not before Avery arrives.

"Just give her a minute," I yell. "Please?"

He sighs. He leans closer so I can hear him over the music. "Emelia, if she falls, she could really get hurt."

While that's true, what he doesn't understand is that she's already really hurt—but this song is hopefully going to fix that.

"Just one more minute?" Violet's already more than halfway through the song, and there's still no sign of Avery. I know that she's here—I saw her parents' Prius in the parking lot. If she doesn't show up soon, then this is all going to have been for nothing. A grand gesture just doesn't have the same impact if you hear about it secondhand.

Mike shakes his head. "Violet better have a very good explanation for this."

And then, all of a sudden, her explanation arrives. Avery is beside me, her cheeks burning.

"What is she doing?" she asks me.

"Trying to win you back."

"'I made too many mistakes, better get this right.'" For the rest of the song, Violet is focused on Avery. Some people in the crowd notice, and they turn around to look at her too. Avery stiffens, and I can feel the embarrassment coming off her in waves.

Maybe this wasn't such a good idea.

Violet's a few beats in front of the music when she finishes singing, but the crowd doesn't seem to notice. Everyone whistles and claps—everyone except Avery.

Violet bows, then lets Alistair help her off the counter.

"All right, show's over, everyone," Mike says. "Back to work." He points at Violet. "Except for you. My office later." He turns and stalks off.

A few people form a line to pay for their items, while the rest of the crowd starts to disperse. Alistair signs into the cash register so he can ring through the customers. Violet walks over to Avery and me, her hands clasped in front of her.

"Wow, Vi," Avery says. "You did great. I can't believe you went to all that trouble."

Violet smiles. "I wanted to do something big. To show you how much you mean to me."

Avery nods, but she doesn't fall into Violet's arms the way we were all hoping she would. Her smile is frozen on her face. It's the kind of look you give someone when you don't know what to say.

I chew my fingernail. Violet doesn't seem to be reading the signals that Avery is sending out—even though they're super obvious—because she takes another step toward her.

"I miss you. And I want to go back to the way things were," Violet says. "I want us back."

"Um, maybe we should go somewhere and talk," Avery replies. "Somewhere a bit more private."

Violet nods. She lets Avery take her by the hand and lead her toward the back of the store. The moment before they disappear down the lighting aisle, Violet glances over her shoulder at me and beams. I smile back, but really, I'm sick inside. Because whatever Avery is about to tell her is not going to be anything that she wants to hear. It's like I'm about to witness a car crash, and there's nothing I can do to stop it from happening. As much as I want to, I can't save Violet from her broken heart.

I can't even save myself.

When I turn around, Alistair is serving the last customer in line. He catches my eye as he hands the man his bag, and this time he doesn't look away. He drums his fingers on the counter as I walk over.

"I think our plan might have backfired," he says, frowning.

Before I can even answer him, Violet runs past us and out through the sliding glass doors. I have no idea how she can move so fast in those boots, but she's like a comet streaking across the sky, her long blond ponytail flying behind her.

"Violet," Avery calls. She runs after her, but stops short at the doors, her face twisted with anguish. She wrings her hands.

"Why would she do something like this?" she says. "I felt like I was really clear with her when we broke up that we're not getting back together."

Alistair and I exchange a nervous glance. We went about this all wrong. Encouraging Violet was obviously a mistake. She needed closure, but maybe she could have gotten that if she'd just talked to Avery.

"It's my fault . . . I may have encouraged her," Alistair says.

Avery's eyes narrow. "What? Why would you do that?"

"He was just trying to help," I say. "We both were."

Avery shakes her head. "Well, thanks, but you've just made things worse."

As I walk past her and push through the doors, I hear her say, "I can't believe you, Al. You're supposed to be on our side!"

Violet's scooter is still in the parking lot, so she couldn't have gone too far. I walk around the building, but she's nowhere to be seen. Then I remember the little park a block away. And that's where I find her, sitting on a picnic table, her face buried in her hands.

For a moment I'm not sure what to do—maybe she'd rather be alone. But she looks up, her face streaked with tears, and I know I can't walk away from her. I know how it feels to want someone you can't have.

I sit down on top of the picnic table beside her.

"I'm such an idiot," she says.

"You're not an idiot. You're brave. Putting yourself out there like that took a lot of courage." I wish I'd found the strength to choose Alistair in the first place.

Violet swipes furiously at the tears on her cheeks. "I should have known that it would turn out this way. I should have listened when she told me we were through. I just . . . didn't want to hear it," she says. "And now I've made a total ass of myself. Why did I think a stupid song would change anything?"

"You have nothing to be embarrassed about."

She shrugs. "She finally admitted that she's with someone, which obviously I already suspected. Still won't tell me who she is, though."

I wonder why Avery is being so secretive about her new girlfriend. I know she doesn't want to hurt Violet any more than she has already, but not telling her who she's dating isn't helping.

"And she said she wants to be friends, but I don't think I can do that. It's too hard."

I get it—boy, do I ever—but I hope that one day they'll find a way to be friends again.

"I'm sorry," I say, resting my hand on her back. "I really hoped things would turn out differently."

A robin lands on the edge of the picnic table. It watches us with its beady black eyes, its head cocked. A warm breeze rustles through the trees.

"Do you want to go home?" I ask her. It would be completely understandable if she wasn't ready to go back in and see Avery. "I can tell Mike you're not feeling well and that I'll take over your shift."

Violet sniffs. "That's okay. I'll be fine."

And she will be. Even if she doesn't truly believe it yet.

"Em?" she says. "Thanks."

I smile. When I changed the past with that crystal, I never imagined that Violet and I would end up friends. I put my arm around her and she leans her head on my shoulder. She's the one thing I don't want to change about my life. I tell myself that if I do manage to track down the palm reader and get a new crystal and change the past again, I won't lose Violet. Whatever happens, I'll make sure that I don't lose her.

✳ CHAPTER ✳
21

Napoleon is waiting at the door for me early the next morning, his leash hanging from his mouth. He's looking at me with such hope and longing that it makes me sigh. I'm still in my pajamas—yoga pants and an old BTS concert T-shirt—but I usually only take him for a quick spin around the block, so who cares if I just rolled out of bed?

But when we get outside, Napoleon is full of energy, tugging the leash in the direction of the dog park. I let him lead me out of our neighborhood and down the street. There's a bit of a bite to the air, the first sign that fall is just around the corner.

The dog park is empty, aside from a woman playing fetch with her golden retriever. I open the metal gate and let Napoleon off his leash. While he bounds across the dewy grass, heading toward a row of shrubs, I sit down on a stone bench.

I'm still trying to track down Irene the palm reader online, but I haven't had any luck finding her. So a few seconds later, when my phone beeps and I see that Violet has sent me a text—*Is this her?*—with a link to a website, my hands start to shake. The link takes me to a website for Art in the Park, an event down by the river where local artists showcase and sell their artwork. I scroll down the site until I find a photo of Irene standing by a series of paintings, all of neon butterflies in various stages of flight.

The next Art in the Park event is tomorrow. I smile. This is a great lead. I know that the same artists don't always show up every weekend, but even if Irene isn't there, one of the other artists might know where I can find her.

The gate squeaks. I look over as Alistair enters the park with Bitsy, the fluffy white powder puff of a dog that he inherited from his grandmother. He spots me and nods, then bends down to unclip the leash from her pink rhinestone collar. Bitsy tears across the field, heading straight for Napoleon.

My cheeks burn. I wish I'd changed out of my ratty old pajamas now. Especially because Alistair looks so hot. He's wearing a white Henley shirt and cargo shorts, a black beanie pulled over his dark curls.

"Hey," he says, walking over and sitting down beside me on the bench.

"Hey."

We watch the dogs run around the park in silence that borders on awkward. There's an undercurrent between us, left over from the other night in his garage. There's so much unsaid—so much that can't be said—that it's affecting the easy way we normally are with each other when we're alone.

I hate this.

Finally, Alistair says, "Have you talked to Violet? I've texted her a few times, but I haven't heard back."

I nod.

"Is she okay?"

"She's about as okay as can be expected after having her heart ripped out."

Alistair shakes his head. "Well, we did warn her."

"Yeah, but we also encouraged her by helping her," I say. "Maybe we shouldn't have meddled."

"We definitely shouldn't have meddled."

"I'm mad at us."

He nods. "Lesson learned, right? Probably best to stay out of your friends' love lives."

"I just wish that Avery would give her another chance." It seems so unfair that Violet put herself out there in such a public way, only to be shot down.

Alistair's knee starts to bounce up and down. "You can't force how you feel, though, right? If Avery doesn't feel it with Violet, she doesn't feel it," he says. "At least now Violet will have the closure she needs to move on."

I sure hope so. Still, I'm annoyed with Avery for not telling Violet who she's seeing. Maybe if Violet knew who the other girl was, it would be easier to accept that Avery is her past, not her future.

"I still don't understand why Avery is keeping her new girlfriend a secret," I say, hoping Alistair will crack and tell me who she is.

He smiles. "I'm not going to tell you who she is, Em. We're staying out of our friends' love lives, remember?"

"That was your idea," I point out.

"All right, well, I'm staying out of it. And this time I mean it," he says. "I've already dug myself a pretty sizable hole by helping Violet with her grand gesture in the first place."

"What do you mean?"

He sighs. "Let's just say that I should have thought things through a little more. Violet's not the only one who got hurt."

Huh? I have no idea what he's talking about. I could push, but I know that I'm not going to get any more out of him on the subject.

The sun comes out. Alistair pulls a pair of aviator sunglasses out of the front pocket of his Henley shirt and slides them on.

"All set for the Catan competition?" The preliminaries are this weekend, and as far as I know, he's still planning on filming them for his USC application.

"I think so. Are you ready?"

I shrug. "I probably haven't practiced as much as I should have." I hope I don't embarrass myself and get knocked out in the first round.

"You don't need much practice anyway," he says.

We lapse into silence again. I think about how things used to be between us, back in the beginning, when we were simply friends. Before all our feelings muddied the waters. And, okay, we're still friends, but it's not the same. It's not easy anymore. I miss how we were. I can't believe that I blew my chance with him, although I'm grateful that he doesn't remember that night.

Soon he won't remember this moment, either, or any of the other moments we've shared recently. Once I get another crystal, all these memories—and all this awkwardness—will be gone. Alistair will never know the lengths I've gone to in order to make things right between us.

But what about Marisol? my conscience whispers.

Alistair is her boyfriend, it's true, but only because I messed with my past. I tell myself that she won't be hurt, because she won't remember that he was ever hers in the first place.

But I'll remember. And I'll have to carry that with me, just like I carry the memory of Alistair's face when I told him I was choosing Ben instead.

* * *

Twenty minutes later, Napoleon and I are coming up the street to my house when I notice the FOR SALE sign on the edge of our lawn. Karen the Realtor must have put it up when I was at the dog park.

I stop short, but Napoleon keeps walking, almost yanking me off my feet.

Seeing that sign in front of my house is a gut punch. It makes everything feel more real. And while I'm planning on turning everything around with a new crystal, I don't know how long it will take to find the palm reader. I'm not anxious to watch my life continue to fall to pieces in the meantime.

I'm almost at my front door when I hear the murmur of my parents' voices floating through the open window.

Wait, Mom's home? She's not supposed to be back from her wellness retreat until tomorrow afternoon. I was going to surprise them by making dinner. I thought maybe if the three of us spent some time together, I'd somehow be able to convince them not to ruin all our lives by breaking up.

I know it's not nice to eavesdrop, but I can't help myself. I move closer to the window, stepping in the garden so I can hear what they're saying. I crouch down, hidden by a bush, so they won't see me.

"Karen doesn't seem to think it'll be on the market long," Dad says.

"Hopefully not," Mom replies. "But in the meantime, we need to figure out our living situation."

"Well, the good news is I got the apartment downtown. I can't move in until the first of the month, but Tom offered to let me stay with him in the meantime. So you're free to stay here at the house until it sells."

My heart sinks. This is really happening. We're really moving.

"No need," Mom says. "I found a rental house in Fairview. Emelia and I can move in right away. I think it's better to be there before school starts. Give her some time to settle in."

My stomach plummets. So not only are we selling our house, but my mom is planning to move me to another town?

I shake my head. I won't do it. I just got Alistair and Marisol back. And, okay, things haven't turned out the way I expected with them, but there's no way I'm going to agree to move away.

"Are you sure about this?" Dad says. "We're already upending

Emelia's life with this divorce. Having her switch schools her senior year, separating her from her friends . . . it seems like a lot to put her through."

"It's not my preference," Mom replies. "But I haven't been able to find anything in town that I can afford on my own. And I'll be closer to work in Fairview, so I'll spend less time commuting. I'm sure Emelia will come around."

My face is hot. Does she even know me? I will not come around.

Napoleon barks, anxious to get inside, and gives me away. The front door suddenly swings open. My mom pokes her head out the door and spots me crouched in the garden.

"Emelia, honey," she says, forcing a smile. I'm sure she's wondering how much of their conversation I overheard. I step out of the garden, trying to keep my rage at this crappy situation in check.

I unclip Napoleon's leash, and he runs past my mom and into the house, almost knocking over her suitcase. My mom moves to hug me, but I sidestep her.

"I'm not moving to Fairview," I say coldly. "And I'm not going to a new school."

She sighs and runs a hand through her newly blond, no-longer-gray hair. This new reality has been good to her—she looks ten years younger than the last time I saw her. She's also tanned, probably thanks to her time in Palm Springs, and more relaxed than I've seen her in ages. All the tennis she's been playing at the wellness retreat shows—her sleeveless white blouse highlights the definition in her arms.

"Let's not get worked up. Nothing's official yet. I'm just throwing ideas around," she says.

But her plans sound pretty final. And I know how my mom is. Once she gets her mind set on something, she'll find a way to make it happen. Moving to Fairview is pretty much a done deal, no matter how I may feel about it.

Unless I can find another crystal.

I relax a little. Maybe she's right—there's no need to get so worked up yet. After all, this is just temporary. None of what's happening right now matters, because it's all going to change anyway once I get my hands on a new crystal. There will be no move, no switching schools. And no divorce.

Mom notices me softening and takes a chance on putting her arms around me. "What are you doing here, anyway?" I ask as she squeezes me. "I thought you weren't coming home until tomorrow."

"I missed you too much to wait another day," she says, kissing my cheek.

I roll my eyes, even though the truth is that I missed her, too. Even if she does want to move me to another town.

"Now, your dad's made French toast, so why don't we go and eat it before it gets cold?"

"I was just about to suggest that," Dad says, grinning at us. He's holding a spatula. He's still in his pajamas, and his dandelion hair is puffier than usual.

I know they're trying to distract me with food—and it usually works. I have to admit that the French toast smells good. And I am hungry.

"Fine," I say. "Just let me wash my hands. They're all dog-parky."

While my parents disappear into the kitchen, I pop into the bathroom. I grimace when I catch sight of my reflection. My hair seriously needs to be brushed, and I have purple bags under my eyes. And there's a coffee stain on my BTS T-shirt that I didn't notice before I left the house.

So it's official—Alistair has seen me at my worst.

Not that it matters, because pretty soon he won't remember how terrible I looked, because this day won't have existed for him. Once I get the crystal and change everything again . . .

But a tiny bit of doubt starts to creep in. What if Irene's not at Art in the Park? What if I never manage to find her?

What if I never actually get another crystal?

What will I do then?

Stop it, I tell myself. I take a few deep breaths to keep myself from spiraling. I'll worry about what to do next if Irene isn't at the art event. Until then, I'm not going to think about it.

When I come out of the bathroom, I can hear the ring of my mom's laughter down the hall. I find my parents seated beside each other, my mom dabbing at her eyes with her napkin.

"I forgot about that," she says.

"Forgot about what?" I sit down across from them and grab a piece of French toast from the platter centered on the table.

She waves her hand. "Just something ridiculous that happened when we were first dating." She starts to laugh again.

Dad gives me a sheepish grin. "It's hard to explain. You kind of had to be there."

Part of me is irritated at their private walk down memory lane, but another part is thrilled that they still have an inside joke. I'd say it's just like old times, but they usually do more bickering than laughing.

I don't quite get why they're getting along so well, now that they've split. It's weird.

"I figured out how to solve our problem," I say as I pour a lake of maple syrup all over my French toast.

"What problem?" Mom asks.

"About where I should live," I reply. "I don't have to move out of town. I can just live with Dad."

Not that I'm actually planning to move, but I need a backup plan, just in case I don't find Irene.

My parents exchange a weighted glance. Dad lowers his fork. "You know that I'd love to have you live with me full-time, Em, but your mom and I have agreed that it would be better for you to stay with her during the week," he says. "I'll be traveling a lot with this new job, and so I won't be around very much."

"That's okay."

He shakes his head. "You're not staying on your own."

"Why not? I'm sixteen!"

"Why don't we table this conversation for now?" Mom says, slipping into corporate-speak. "We can revisit it when we sell the house."

What she really means is that this conversation is over. I don't have a choice in the matter. I'll be moving to Fairview with her.

Well, I'm not about to sit here and eat French toast with

them like everything's fine. They can pretend that we're all still a happy family if they want, but I'm not going to.

I jump up and run out of the kitchen.

"Emelia," my mom calls as I head upstairs.

I slam my bedroom door, then throw open my closet doors and pull out the boxes I just packed the other day. I remove the chili-pepper lights and string them back up around the window. I tack my Cuba poster back above my bed. I tack the photos of Marisol, Alistair, and me back on the bulletin board, where they belong.

I survey my put-back-together room and let out a breath.

I'm not going anywhere.

✳ CHAPTER ✳
22

I get up the next morning and head to the park. The Catan competition is in a few hours, but I have something important to do first. I slip my crystal into the pocket of my hoodie and head down to the river.

The gravel path that leads to the park is busier than usual. A bunch of artists are set up on the grass, selling watercolor paintings, pottery, and handmade jewelry, but despite the crowds, I spot Irene, my palm reader, right away. My fingers tighten around the crystal. She's sitting at a folding table covered with a red cloth. Her deck of tarot cards is set in front of her, along with a clay bowl of different-colored stones that shine in the morning sunlight. She's surrounded by paintings of butterflies on easels.

I let out a deep breath, my shoulders relaxing.

I found her. Finally.

Everything is going to be all right.

I walk toward her and Irene glances up as I approach her table.

"Good morning." She smiles, her translucent blue eyes crinkling up at the corners. She's wearing a flowing green caftan, and her long white hair is pulled back in a French braid.

"Morning." I smile at her, but she doesn't recognize me, of course—in this reality, we've never met.

Despite all the time I've spent looking for her, I don't quite know how to start this conversation, so I just open my fingers and show her the crystal.

Her smile deepens. "Ooh, rutilated quartz. A very powerful stone."

"Yes, you've told me that before."

She leans back in her chair and studies me. "Ah. So, did it work for you?"

"Yes," I reply. "But not like I expected it to. Nothing has turned out the way I expected it to."

She nods. "Your sweater unraveled, then. Well, I'm sure I must have warned you about that."

"Yes, you did, but—"

Irene's eyes suddenly narrow. "Wait. You didn't try to raise the dead, did you?"

I shake my head and her face relaxes. "Oh, good," she says. "I know I must have warned you against doing that, but you'd be surprised how many people don't listen."

"I'm hoping that you can help me."

She frowns and holds up a finger. "No refunds. I know I must have told you that."

"I don't want a refund," I say. "I want another stone. I want another chance to make things right." I sift through the bowl of crystals—jade, amethyst, emerald.

"I don't have any more rutilated quartz. You got the last one," she says, and a chill settles over me. "Not that it matters. The crystal doesn't work like that, anyway. You can't keep going back. It's a one-shot deal." She points to the butterfly paintings behind her. "Do you know about the butterfly effect?"

"Vaguely."

"Chaos theory," she says. "Basically, the idea is that a small change in the atmosphere, like a butterfly flapping its wings in Brazil, can cause catastrophic consequences somewhere else, like a hurricane in Japan. Make the tiniest change or decision in one area of your life and it can have a huge effect on the rest of your life."

Like choosing Ben over Alistair. That decision had a ripple effect on everything, even if I'll never know exactly how. Guilt stabs at my chest. My decision to go back and change things with Alistair has already affected my friends and family, but maybe going back and changing things again will fix that. Maybe my parents will be back together.

"So, is there somewhere else that I can buy another crystal?"

"Afraid not," Irene says, sighing. "I got that particular rock from a cave deep in the Australian outback years ago. I don't have any more."

And she was willing to sell it to me for fifteen dollars?

As if she can read my mind—although maybe she can?—

Irene says, "I only sold those crystals to people who truly seemed to need it." She shrugs. "I must have thought you fit the bill."

I bite my lip. "But . . . how am I supposed to fix everything, then?"

She smiles, but she doesn't give me an answer. She holds up the old, weathered deck of tarot cards, their corners lifted with use. "Why don't I do a reading for you? On the house."

She gestures for me to take the plastic chair across from her. I sit down as she knocks her knuckles against the deck, then hands the cards to me.

"Shuffle them eight times," she says. "It's important that you put your vibe on them. And make sure you're thinking of your question."

I close my eyes. There are so many things that I want to change, but I silently ask, *How do I fix my life?*—hoping that will cover all of it. When I'm done shuffling the cards, I open my eyes. Irene instructs me to divide the deck into three piles on the table, so I cut the cards into three neat stacks.

"Now turn over the top card on each pile, starting with the one on the left," she says. "These cards represent your past, present, and future."

I flip over the first card, the one that's supposed to signify my past. It's a winged red devil with a pointy black beard, two horns curling out of his head like a ram. At his feet are a man and a woman. They're totally naked except for the thick chains looped around their necks that bind them together.

My stomach drops. That can't be good.

"Ah," Irene says. "The Devil. Desire and lust, temptation and unhealthy relationships." She stares pointedly at me. "This card is telling us that you made the wrong choice sometime in the past."

I blink at her, stunned. All right, so that's weirdly accurate.

She motions for me to move on to the next card, the one that tells of my present. My hands shake slightly as I turn it over. This one is a black-and-white illustration of a court jester about to walk off the edge of a cliff. I gasp. It looks exactly like the joker cards I found at the night market and in front of her old store, Mystic Moon.

My hands start to shake. "I keep finding this card everywhere."

Irene nods. "That makes sense. The joker—or the Fool, in tarot—can represent new beginnings and having faith in the future. The Fool is telling you to shed your emotional baggage, heal past hurts, and start fresh."

Okay . . . but how exactly am I supposed to do that? Letting go of the past is easier said than done. I frown. And does starting fresh refer to selling our house and going to a new school?

I flip over the final card, the one that's supposed to predict my future. It turns out my future is a freaky-looking skeleton in a suit of armor, sitting atop a white horse with red eyes.

"Ooh, Death," Irene says, leaning forward.

I flinch. Why did I think this reading was a good idea?

"Before you start worrying, it's not death in the literal sense," she adds, and I let out a breath. "It simply indicates a change in your future. This card is showing us that you're coming into a time of significant transformation and transition. Something has to end in order for something new to begin."

Irene taps a finger against her lips. "You know, it's interesting . . . these are all Major Arcana. They signify life lessons or major events, huge changes and emotions," she says. "If we look at your spread altogether, I think the message is that whatever the mistake is that you feel you made in the past, you need to put it to rest. You have to move on. This is your chance to be the best version of yourself. Does that make sense?"

I nod warily. I think she's telling me that I need to let go of the idea that Alistair and I will ever be together. Without another crystal, Alistair and I will never be together. Without that crystal, I'm stuck in this reality, the one where I'll have to split my time between my parents' houses and start a new school, away from my friends.

"Don't look so discouraged," Irene says, leaning over and patting my hand. "Believe it or not, this was a good reading. I think you're going to be pleasantly surprised with how everything turns out."

Maybe. Or maybe I'm going to spend the rest of my life wishing that I'd left well enough alone. If I hadn't bought that stupid crystal, Alistair and Marisol wouldn't be together, and I'd be in Italy right now with my still-together parents, walking the cobblestone streets eating gelato. Of course, I'd still be wishing I had my friends back and torn about breaking up with Ben, but who knows, maybe I would have eventually found the courage to dump him. And maybe Alistair would have eventually forgiven me and we would have had a shot, if I'd just told him how I was feeling.

But now I guess I'll never know.

✳ CHAPTER ✳
23

Finding out that there's nothing I can do to change my past and I'm stuck with my life as it is, even if Irene claims that everything is going to turn out great, puts me in a terrible mood. The last thing I feel like doing is playing in the Catan competition, but I promised Alistair I'd be there. He needs me for his documentary. So, half an hour later, I meet him and Violet outside Bonus Round. Violet's already wearing the bright yellow wristband that marks her as a player.

"Afternoon," Alistair says, handing me an identical wristband. "I signed you in. There are eighty-four people registered, so you'll have your work cut out for you to get to the semifinals."

I slip the wristband on. "Where's Marisol?" I know she decided not to play in the tournament, but I was hoping she'd come anyway, for moral support. Catan has always been our game, after all.

"She said she wasn't up for it," Alistair says.

She hasn't been up for much lately. She's been so distant. It's just not like her. I really hope she hasn't figured out that I have feelings for Alistair.

Alistair holds open the door and we head inside. Bonus Round is crammed with a lot of familiar faces—all the regulars have come out to try to win one of the coveted seats in the semifinals. The nervous energy in the air is totally contagious, and my palms start to sweat. I haven't really taken this tournament that seriously, but now I feel my competitive nature kicking in.

I want to win. I *need* to win at something.

The first game is supposed to start in five minutes, and most of the players are hovering near the numbered tables, anxiously waiting for the host to tell them that they can sit down. Twenty-one Catan boards are spread out on top of red tablecloths, dice resting on top, piles of resource cards neatly stacked and ready to be claimed.

"You're at table thirteen," Alistair says to me. "Violet's at seven. I'm going to go back and forth between you. Remember, don't look at the camera. Just pretend I'm not here."

My nerves are next-level at the thought of being on camera, and I feel added pressure to play well so his documentary turns out okay.

Josh, one of the baristas at Bonus Round and a Dungeons and Dragons local legend, steps over to a mic at the front of the room. He's tall and thin, with wheat-blond hair that reminds me of the bales of hay stacked in farmers' fields every spring.

"Welcome to the Catan preliminaries!" Josh says.

There's a round of applause, a rise of excitement in the room.

"We'll be playing three rounds of Catan today. The outcome of these games will determine which sixteen players will advance to the semifinals." He goes on to explain that semifinalists will be invited back to play one game tomorrow morning, and those sixteen players will be whittled down to four players, who will then compete in the final game tomorrow afternoon.

"And the winner of the final will, of course, be awarded a seat in the Catan United States Championship being held in September in Ohio!"

Another round of applause. Alistair's busy filming Josh's speech on his phone, but he catches me stealing a look at him and he smiles.

"Before we get started, a few housekeeping details." Josh runs through a list of rules, most of which are basic common sense—no harassing other players, no trash talk, no physical contact—then he smiles and invites the players to sit down at our tables.

"Good luck, Em," Violet says.

"You too."

I weave through the crowd to table thirteen, Alistair following behind me.

I sit down at the table. The other three players are an older man, an eleven-year-old girl, and one of the college guys I've seen playing Dungeons and Dragons with Josh. A whistle blows from somewhere, the signal that we can start the game.

After a few turns, I realize that I've got this on lock. I'm three points ahead within the first twenty minutes, building cities and settlements like a boss. My main competition is the eleven-year-old, but even she quickly falls behind.

Forty-five minutes later, I'm at ten points. I've won the first game. I glance up at Alistair. I've been so focused that I forgot all about him and his camera. He beams at me as I shake hands with the other players.

There's a short break before the next game. While Josh and his friends set up the boards again, Violet wanders over and the three of us head to the counter for a drink.

"So, that was intense," Violet says, pushing a straw through the lid on her iced tea. "I barely made it through that round."

"You still won."

"By one point. And only because I got lucky and pulled the university card." She nudges Alistair. "Did you get some good footage?"

He nods. "I have to edit it all down to ten minutes, so I'm trying not to shoot too much. I just want to capture the most important moments."

We finish our drinks just as Josh posts the new seating chart on the wall. Alistair pushes through the crowd to check which tables Violet and I will be playing at. In order to get to the semi-finals, we both need to win the next two games. And that means we need to be playing at different tables again—because if we're in the same game and one of us wins, we'll knock the other one out.

Alistair returns a minute later. He smiles. "Em, you're at table two. Violet, table four."

Violet and I high-five for good luck and then move in opposite directions. This time, Alistair follows her.

I stop short as I reach my table. Drew, Ben's best friend, the guy who tormented Alistair in middle school and sucker punched him at the night market, is at my table.

A Catan competition is the last place I'd ever expect to run into Drew Halvorsen. Even stranger, he's with Matt and Aiden, two gamers from my school who Drew normally wouldn't be caught dead with. And yet, from the way they're all joking around, it seems that they're friends.

I'm confused, but then it dawns on me—Drew has been cast out of Ben's group. His tumble down the social ladder must be related to Ben and Olivia's relationship. It's the only explanation.

I can't help but smile. It couldn't have happened to a better person. I guess there's one good thing that came out of me messing around with that crystal.

"Hi." I sit down beside Drew. He glances at me with a polite expression. "How did you guys end up at the same table?"

"Lucky draw," Drew says, but Aiden snickers. "Emelia, right?"

Ah, yes. Thanks to the crystal, Drew won't remember that we have a history. He has no idea that I've been to his house and swum in his pool or that I've seen him throw up after drinking one too many beers too many times to count.

"Weren't you in my English class last year?" he asks me.

"Yup." I sat behind him in different classes for years before Ben and I started dating and Drew was forced to acknowledge my existence.

He's wearing a T-shirt with a cartoon beaver and THERE'S NO PLACE I'D RATHER BE THAN BEAVER VALLEY written on it, so how much has he changed, really?

A tiny part of me wonders what would happen if I started dropping intimate details of his life. How badly would that freak him out?

I laugh to myself. I'm super tempted to mess with him, but I guess I should focus my attention on the game. If I somehow lost to Drew, I would never get over it.

The whistle blows. We roll the dice and Drew has the highest number. After he's placed his first road and settlement, we go around the circle until all of us are on the board and the game officially starts.

Drew rolls a six. As it turns out, I needn't have worried about him being an actual contender. He stares at the game board, confused, until Matt instructs that he pick up an ore card. Technically, this is a competition—Matt's not supposed to be giving him any hints—but I'll let it slide because there's no way Drew is going to win. In order to even be at this table, he must have won his first game, but I have no idea how he managed to pull that off.

"What do I do with this card again?" he asks.

I sigh inwardly. He must be pretty desperate for human interaction to enter a tournament when he doesn't really know how to play the game. Not that he's taking any of this seriously. Despite the rule about no trash-talking, that's pretty much all Drew does, tossing out insults and laughing so loud the other players turn to look—so no different from how he used to act.

It's distracting, more for Matt and Aiden than for me, which is how I end up winning the second game by six points in just under half an hour.

"Well, that was a waste of a Saturday," Drew says. He leans back in his chair, the back two legs lifting off the floor. "Why did I let you guys talk me into this?"

The tips of Matt's ears begin to turn red. "We didn't talk you into anything—you wanted to come."

Drew scoffs. "Well, now I want to leave. This is seriously lame." He lets the legs of his chair drop back to the floor with a thud and stands up. "Let's get out of here."

Aiden shrugs and he follows Drew outside. Matt sighs but he stands up too.

"Good luck," he says to me.

As he's walking away, it hits me—Matt is me. Or was me, when I was hanging out with Ben and his friends. Always going along with what the group wanted, afraid to rock the boat in case they decided to throw me off it.

I get up and walk over to Alistair. He's standing a few feet away from Violet's table, trying to blend in to the background so she won't notice him filming her. I don't think he needs to worry—she seems to be lost in the game. Violet pulls on her lower lip, concentrating on the board. She's playing against a middle-aged man, an older lady, and the hipster guy who works at the bike shop down the street.

As the games around us begin to wrap up and people start to get up and move around the room, I'm pushed closer and closer to Alistair until eventually our shoulders are touching.

It's just shoulder contact, which is really no big deal, aside from the fact that it lights me up inside. I've stood shoulder to shoulder with him a million times before, but it's never felt sparky like this. Somewhere along the way, things changed between us. And I don't know how to go back to thinking of Alistair as just a friend. The worst part is, I don't really want to.

Twenty minutes later, Violet wins her second game. She does the *V* for *Victory* sign—or maybe it's *V* for *Violet*. Either way, with two wins under her belt, she now has a pretty solid shot at making the semifinals.

"I'm assuming you won," she says to me.

"You assume right."

She rubs her hands together. "Just one more game to go."

After another brief break to reset the boards, Josh posts the seating chart for the third game. Alistair goes to check the tables Violet and I will be playing at. When he comes back a minute later, I can tell from the look on his face that he doesn't have good news.

"You're both at table seven," he says.

"Crap," Violet replies.

Yeah, crap. Being at the same table means only one of us can win a seat at the semifinals.

This sucks.

"Maybe they'll let us switch," Violet says.

Alistair shakes his head. "Josh would never allow that."

The game is about to start, so Violet and I take our seats at table seven. We wish each other luck, but I know that I'm not going to need it. I've been playing Catan forever, and I'm not going to give up a seat in the semifinals. Violet may be my friend, but she is about to go down.

Hipster Guy is at our table. He sighs as he sits down beside Violet.

"Brent," he says, nodding at me.

"Emelia."

Lindsay, one of the baristas at Bonus Round, slips into the seat next to me. The game starts. I manage to gain a one-point lead early on, thanks to a good hand of resource cards that allow me to upgrade one of my first settlements to a city. I'm vaguely aware of Alistair standing over my shoulder, but I try to block him out.

Violet rolls a seven and Brent groans. Seven is the robber, a gray game piece that can be used to block another player from receiving resources. It also means that any players with more than seven resource cards—in this case, me and Brent—have to return half our cards to the bank. And there go the cards I need to buy another city.

Violet picks up the gray game piece, letting it hover over the board as she tries to decide where to relocate it. Her eyes flick to me, and she smiles as she sets the piece squarely beside one of my hexes. And then she steals one of my lumber cards.

Oh, now it's on.

Half an hour later, Brent and Lindsay are in my rearview mirror, but Violet and I are tied at nine points. Part of the game strategy is to keep your cards hidden so the other players don't know what you're holding. I have no idea what cards Violet has, but I just need one more grain card and I'll be able to buy a city. And that city will push me to ten points.

I'm so close to winning this game.

As it turns out, luck is with me, and on Brent's next turn, he rolls a four. Violet and I each have settlements that border the hex marked four—which also happens to be a grain hex. I try to keep my face expressionless as Brent hands each of us a grain card from the bank, although inside I'm bubbling with excitement.

Lindsay's up next, but I don't pay much attention to what she's doing. I'm practically bouncing up and down in my seat, ready for my turn. I'm anxious to trade my resource cards in for a city and put an end to this game and secure my seat in the semifinals, but then I make the mistake of looking over at Violet. From the way she's staring intently at her cards and chewing her bottom lip in an effort not to smile, I know that she's also got the cards she needs to win this game.

Only that's not going to happen. Because it's my turn.

I hesitate.

The old Emelia had a ruthless, take-no-prisoners, win-at-all-costs approach, at least when it came to board games—and maybe that extended to other parts of my life too. But now . . . now I'm not so sure that I want to win if it means that Violet will lose. She's still reeling over what happened with Avery— winning this game and a seat in the semifinals might help make her feel better.

I think about Irene the palm reader, and how she said I'll have the opportunity to be better. Maybe this is where I start.

And so, instead of buying another city, I roll the dice.

"Ten," Lindsay says. "No one's beside that hex, so I guess it's over to you, Violet."

The smile Violet was trying to hold back spreads across her face. She slaps down her lumber, brick, grain, and wool cards and buys a settlement from the bank, which tips her over to ten points and wins her the game.

She whoops and jumps out of her seat, hands in the air. Okay, so she's not exactly the most gracious winner, especially when she starts dancing around the table, but I laugh anyway. I'm glad to see her so happy.

As she's swallowed by a crowd of onlookers, Alistair leans over my shoulder and whispers in my ear. His breath is warm on my neck, sending a shiver through me.

"I saw your cards. You could have won," he says. "You threw the game."

I shake my head. "I don't know what you're talking about."

I can't see Alistair's face, but I can hear the smile in his voice as he says, "What have you done with Emelia?"

I smile. She's still here. She's just a new, upgraded version. Emelia 2.0.

Violet dances back to our table. She points to her name, already spelled out in wooden tiles on the giant Scrabble board along with the other fifteen players who will compete in tomorrow's semifinals.

"Congratulations, Vi," I say, standing up to give her a hug.

She throws her arms around my neck. "I can't believe it. I won! I beat you!"

"Yeah, yeah, okay," I say. "No trash-talking, remember?"

She laughs. "Sorry, sorry. Will you guys come and watch me play in the semifinals?"

"Of course," I say.

"Wouldn't miss it." Alistair's eyes meet mine. As Violet squeezes me again, he smiles at me. I may not have won a seat at the semifinals, but I feel like I've won something even better.

✳ CHAPTER ✳
24

Alistair and I offer to take Violet anywhere she wants to go to celebrate her win at the Catan preliminaries. She wants to go to the night market, even though it's miserable outside, so we kill time at her house for a few hours until the market opens. And that's how we find ourselves waiting for tornado potatoes, wearing the clear plastic ponchos that she brought to keep us from getting completely soaked.

"I told you this is the best time to be here," Violet says, smiling. "No lines."

"That's because no one else is willing to risk being struck by lightning just for a baked potato." Alistair wipes at the rain dripping down his face. There's only so much a poncho can do, especially when it's the wrong size. The hood doesn't quite cover his head, and the front of his hair is wet and sticking to his forehead. Violet and I have managed to stay pretty dry, all things considered.

Violet tsks. "It's a *spiral* potato," she says. "And trust me, you'll be singing a different tune once you try it."

I glance at her. I mean, the potatoes are good, but she might be overselling them a little. I'm not sure they're worth walking around in soggy sneakers for.

We eat them huddled under an empty tent, listening to the rain drum against the canvas roof. There are quite a few empty booths—I guess those vendors must have decided that it wasn't worth it to show up in this weather—and most of the rides are closed. I'm hoping that Violet will want to leave after we finish eating, but she's determined to walk around.

I'm shivering as we follow her through the nearly empty market, dodging puddles. Despite the rain, it still feels festive—the air smells like mini doughnuts, and the neon signs for the rides and carnival games are all lit up, casting a rainbow glow over everything.

I haven't been here since the night I came back to find the palm reader. My breath hitches. I don't know how I'm going to make peace with the fact that there's no going back. It's hard to accept that my parents are getting divorced and that my mom and I are moving, all because I interfered with fate. If I'd just left everything alone, then I wouldn't be in this situation.

And then there's Alistair . . .

We're stopped in front of a booth offering temporary tattoos. The rain has let up a little and he's pushed his hood off. There's no one around us, but he's standing as close to me as if we're in the middle of a crowd. His arm brushes against mine more times than can be considered accidental, and every time, I feel that touch through my entire body.

The upside to changing my past is that I'm here with him. Things may not have turned out the way that I thought they would, but I'm still glad to have him back in my life.

Even if it means that he belongs to someone else.

My chest feels tight at the thought of never being more than friends with him. It's torture to think of him with Marisol and not with me, and I know that makes me a terrible person. Not so terrible that I would ever do anything to come between them, but terrible just the same.

I had my chance with him. And I blew it. I have to accept that.

Violet ends up getting a fake tattoo of the Dark Mark on the inside of her arm. Her finger hovers over the glittering green skull with a snake protruding out of its mouth. "You think if I press it I'll be able to summon Avery?" she asks.

I give her a look. "Come on, Vi," I say. "I know you're mad at her, but she's not Voldemort. She didn't set out to hurt you."

She harrumphs. "I was only kidding."

Alistair and I exchange a weary glance. By unspoken agreement, we've avoided bringing up anything that might make her think of Avery—I'd hoped that would be enough to keep her out of Violet's thoughts, at least for tonight.

Now that we're on the subject, I wait for her to press him again about Avery's new girlfriend, but to my surprise, she just grabs my hand and drags me toward the ring toss.

"No one ever wins at these games, Vi. They're rigged," I say, but she's already pulling out her wallet. She slaps a ten-dollar bill down on the counter, and the bored-looking guy manning the booth sets three plastic rings in front of her.

Violet shakes out her hands and rolls her neck. She flicks her wrist, chucking the first plastic ring like a Frisbee. It lands perfectly around the neck of the soda bottle. She must be some kind of ring-toss superhero, because she repeats this a bunch more times, until the guy pulls a giant unicorn down from the zoo of stuffed animals dangling from the ceiling and gives it to her.

Violet smiles. Then she turns and thrusts the unicorn into Alistair's arms. "For you."

"Oh, um." He blinks, his brow furrowing in confusion. "Don't you want to keep it?"

She shakes her head. "Nope. I won it for you."

"Okay. Well." He stares into the glassy blue eyes of the unicorn. "Thanks?"

I bite the inside of my cheek so I won't laugh. It's a sweet gesture, but the idea of Alistair carrying this enormous unicorn around for the rest of the night strikes me as funny—knowing Violet, she only gave it to him because she didn't want to be stuck lugging it around herself. Alistair catches me trying to hold my laughter in and pokes me in the side.

When it starts to rain again, Alistair shrugs out of his poncho and puts it on his unicorn, which makes Violet and me howl. He's soaked to the skin when we finally leave the night market and climb into his mom's minivan. Violet and I take off our ponchos.

We drop Violet off at her house first.

She's about to get out when she leans over from the back seat and gives each of us a hug. "Thanks, guys," she says.

Alistair makes sure Violet's inside her house before he backs out of her driveway. Now that she's gone and we're alone, there's a charge to the air that's hard to ignore. I sneak a look at him and my heart starts to race. He's staring at the road ahead, but I know from the way he's gripping the wheel that he's as aware of me as I am of him. Feelings are flying everywhere, but they have nowhere to go. We can't be together. Neither of us would ever do that to Marisol.

I only live a couple of blocks from Violet, so it doesn't take long before we're on my street and Alistair's pulling up to the curb in front of my house. Right in front of the FOR SALE sign.

My stomach drops. I forgot about the sign. *How could I forget about the sign?*

"Em," he says, turning to look at me. I stare at the windshield wipers moving back and forth so that I don't have to look at him. "Are you moving?"

I let out a long breath, my fingers plucking at the hem of my shirt. "I was going to mention it . . ."

Alistair waits for me to finish my sentence.

"But?" he finally prompts.

I shrug. "I didn't know how to tell you."

"Okay. So, where are you moving? Somewhere in town, right?"

When I don't answer him, he rests his hand on my arm. I know that he wants me to look at him, but I can't do it. I am this close to breaking down.

"Are you . . . moving away?" he asks.

I nod. "To Fairview. With my mom."

"What about your dad?"

"He found an apartment in town."

My throat closes. I'm expecting sympathy that my parents have split up, I'm expecting him to be upset that I'm leaving— what I'm not expecting is for him to get mad at me.

"I can't believe this," Alistair says, raking a hand through his still-damp hair. "Were you ever planning to tell me or were you just going to take off in the middle of the night?"

His sharp tone makes me bristle. He has no right to be upset with me. He's not the one who has to move, after all. He's not the one who's going to have to spend his senior year at a new school.

He'll still be here. With Marisol.

I'm suddenly consumed with white-hot jealousy. Everything is working out for them, but nothing is working out for me, and I hate my life. And if I don't get out of this van right now, I'm going to explode.

I unbuckle my seat belt, struggling not to cry as I throw open the door. Alistair calls after me as I jump out of the van and speed-walk across the grass, the rain soaking me. I can't handle his feelings right now—I can barely handle my own.

He swears, and a second later I hear him open his door and then the sound of footsteps as he runs after me.

"Em, will you just stop for a second," he says.

I spin around. Everything is rushing to the surface, and I can't stop it. I'm too far gone. "What do you want from me, Alistair?"

He blinks, taken aback. Somehow I've flipped the conversation on him. "What do you mean?"

"I mean, what do you want from me?" I wrap my arms around myself as the rain pours down around us.

He blushes. I've caught him off guard, and he's at a total loss for words.

"You have a girlfriend!" I yell.

His head snaps back as if I've slapped him. "It's not—I don't—"

But I don't let him finish. I stomp inside my house and slam the door. I don't want to hear anything he has to say. Deep down, I know that being angry at him isn't fair, that I'm coming at him with this out of nowhere, but I can't help myself.

"Emelia?" Dad says as I kick off my wet sneakers. He and my mom are watching TV together in the living room, as you do when you're getting divorced.

I scowl. What is wrong with them? They're acting like best friends. They're getting along better than they ever have, so I don't understand why they can't just stay together. Why do they have to completely upend my life?

I don't want to talk to them. I don't want to be around them. I just want to be alone.

I run up the stairs and into my room. Through my window, I see Alistair leaning against the van, typing something into his phone. A second later, my phone buzzes. He wants me to come back outside and talk, but I can't do it. I don't even know what to say to him. I'm already starting to feel stupid for losing control of my emotions. My behavior pretty much just confirmed that

I'm into him. Despite promising myself that I'd never get in the way of his relationship with Marisol, I went ahead and told him anyway.

I haven't changed at all. I'm still the same selfish person I've always been. I'm still all about me.

I shut my blinds and flop down face-first on my bed. And a few minutes later, I hear Alistair start the van and drive away.

✳ CHAPTER ✳
25

I need to talk to Marisol.

I should probably wait until morning, once I've calmed down, but I'm full of nervous energy, and even though it's late, there's no way I'm going to be able to sleep if I don't hear her voice.

I have to let her know that I'm moving, before Alistair gets to her. I can only hope that he keeps his mouth shut until I have the chance to tell her myself.

God. I put my head in my hands. I've messed everything up again. I don't know how I'm going to face him after what I said. Knowing that he knows how I feel about him is excruciating. I don't know how to backpedal from this. It's out there, and this time there's no going back.

I take a deep breath and send Marisol a text, but twenty minutes later I still haven't heard from her. I'm going to have to go over to her house so that I can talk to her in person. Since my parents definitely won't be cool with me being out after curfew, I have to wait another half an hour until they go to bed—Mom in what used to be their room, Dad in the guest room—before I pull on a hoodie and sneak downstairs.

The rain has stopped, but there's still a chill in the air. I'm almost at Marisol's house when I spot Alistair's mom's van parked next door in his driveway. All the lights are off at his house. I know his mom and sister are still on their camping trip, so he's either already asleep or he's over at Marisol's.

I pause. Of course he's at Marisol's. Why wouldn't he be? She's his girlfriend. I just hope that he's not telling her my news—or anything else that happened tonight.

My insides curdle. What if Alistair tells her that I'm into him? I don't think he would do that, but I'm only about 98 percent sure. The other 2 percent is worried.

I chew my fingernail. I can't take the risk that he's at Marisol's house—I'm so not ready to see him—so I change course. Violet lives one street over. Maybe it will help to talk things out with her first. And I need to tell her that I'm moving, too. Might as well get it over with.

I shoot her a quick text as I walk, to let her know that I'm dropping by, but I haven't heard back from her by the time I reach her house. I'm walking up the path when the front door flies open.

Violet's standing in the doorway and she's glaring at me. Her eyes are red and puffy. "Did you know?"

"Did I know about what?" I ask, confused. "Why are you looking at me like you want to kill me?"

"Swear that you didn't know," she says.

"Vi, I have no idea what you're talking about."

She crosses her arms. "Avery and Marisol."

"What about them?"

"*Avery* and *Marisol*," she repeats, and I finally get what it is that she's trying to tell me.

Marisol is Avery's secret girlfriend.

WHAT?

My heart starts to pound. "Are you sure?"

"Avery just left," she says, her shoulders slumping. "She came over to tell me."

I have so many questions. Starting with:

"So Marisol and Alistair aren't together?"

She shakes her head. "He was just covering for them. I guess Marisol asked him to pretend to be her boyfriend so that no one would suspect anything. Apparently, Marisol wasn't ready to tell everyone," she says. "But something must have happened, because Alistair just informed them that he wasn't going to go along with it anymore."

My head is spinning. A bunch of conflicting feelings rush at me all at once—relief and happiness that he isn't Marisol's boyfriend, and never has been, and hurt that they didn't let me in on their secret. I can't believe she would keep something like this from me. And, okay, I know I don't really have any right to be upset with her—there are plenty of things that I haven't told her—but Alistair could have said something.

Alistair. Why did he agree to go along with this? And, more important, why did he tell her that he isn't going to anymore?

I swallow. I think I already know the answer to that. I think it's because of me. Because of what I said to him tonight. Because now he knows that I like him. And I think he still likes me, too.

"That's good news for you, right?" Violet says, as if she can hear my thoughts.

"Um, what?" I laugh nervously. "Why would that be good news?"

She rolls her eyes. "Come on, Em. I've seen you guys together. It's totally obvious that you're into him."

Oh God. It's obvious?

I think about denying it, but what's the point. She's onto me.

"Look, it doesn't even matter, because I'm moving," I say, all the happiness and hope I'd felt just a moment before yanked out from under me. I'm beginning to think that fate is conspiring to keep us apart.

I tell Violet about my parents splitting up and my mom's plans to move us to Fairview.

"I already know how Alistair feels about long-distance relationships—according to him, they never work."

Violet snorts. "Fairview's, like, half an hour away. That's not exactly Mars."

"It might as well be."

"Why don't you let him make that decision?" she says. "Stop talking yourself out of this, Em. You're just afraid."

Of course I'm afraid. I'm flat-out terrified.

There's still that voice in my head, the one that worries what will happen if we try this and we don't work out. I can't turn back the clock this time. Like everyone else on earth, I have to live with the consequences of my decisions.

And what if I've read all the signs wrong? Alistair may have confessed his feelings for me the first time around, but he hasn't really given me any concrete proof that he feels that way now. Not really.

"What if . . . ," I start.

"You tell him how you feel and he doesn't feel the same way?" she finishes. "You're not going to know unless you try. Wondering what might have been is way worse than taking a chance." She gives me a small smile. "You know, even if I knew that things would end the way they did with Avery, I'd still do it all over again."

She's right, of course. I mean, this is why I used the crystal in the first place. I wanted a do-over, a second chance. And now I have it.

I may not be able to change my past, but I can still change my future.

I just need to be brave enough to take the leap.

✳ CHAPTER ✳
26

The lights are still off at Alistair's house, aside from one dim beam that shines on the front porch. Alistair's sitting on the porch swing, looking at something on his phone as I walk up his driveway on legs that feel like they're made of water.

He glances at me as I climb the stairs.

"Of all the gin joints in all the towns in all the world, she walks into mine," he says. I'm sweating and my breath is coming in short bursts, like I've just run a marathon. Or I'm hyperventilating.

I'm really going to do this. I'm really going to tell him how I feel.

He stops the swing so I can sit down beside him, then waits until I'm settled before he pushes his foot against the floor, sending it swaying gently back and forth again. If I slid over, just the tiniest bit, our legs would be touching. That little bit of space is the only thing separating us, the line that we need to cross to go from being friends into something more, but I'm so nervous that I can't make myself move any closer.

"Why didn't you tell me about Marisol?" I ask him.

He sighs. "I promised her I wouldn't tell anyone. If I'd thought for one minute that there was a chance that you—"

"If you're a bird, I'm a bird," I interrupt him.

"What?"

"I could be fun, if you want. I could be . . ." I frown. Shoot, what is the line? "Smart! Or superstitious or . . . something else," I ramble, my heart dangerously close to pounding right out of my chest. "The bottom line is, I can be whatever you want."

Alistair is quiet for a minute. "Are you butchering a quote from *The Notebook*?"

"Yes."

"Why?"

He doesn't remember quoting that same passage to me, of course, that night in the snow. He doesn't remember anything about the first time around, and I'm suddenly so grateful that the crystal actually worked, because now I have the chance to make this right.

"Because it's you. It's always been you." And deep down, I know that it always has. I was just too blinded by Ben and my desire to be part of the popular crowd to see it.

Alistair moves closer, closing that last bit of distance between us. His face is inches from mine, so close that I can feel his breath. His nose brushes against mine. "Are you sure?" he whispers.

I nod. I've never been more sure of anything.

He slides his hand across my cheek, his fingers tangling in my hair, and then finally, FINALLY, Alistair—my childhood friend, my something more—kisses me.

And you want to know who doesn't suck at kissing?

Spoiler alert: It's Alistair Stewart.

✳ CHAPTER ✳
27

"All right, just remember, this isn't the final cut," Alistair says. "I'm still not finished editing yet."

It's been a week since the Catan finals and we're back in Marisol's basement, about to screen Alistair's documentary. He's been locked up in his room for the past two days working on it, but I managed to coax him into taking a break—and Marisol somehow twisted his arm into showing us his film.

Alistair plugs the cord into his phone. He's already warned me that he's chosen to focus the story on Violet—which makes sense, since she won the Catan tournament. She'll be heading to Ohio in the fall to compete in the Catan United States Championship.

He presses play and the screen lights up with an exterior shot of Bonus Round, the final day of the tournament. He walks over and plunks down next to me on the futon, putting his arm around my shoulders. I settle into the crook of his arm, a place that feels made just for me. Marisol smiles at us. After the news about her and Avery broke, she apologized for keeping me in the dark about their relationship, and I apologized for not telling her about my parents' divorce, our house being up for sale, and the fact that I'm probably moving. I'm so glad that there are no more secrets between us and our friendship is back on track.

"I really didn't expect to win," on-screen Violet says over a slow-motion shot of her leaping out of her chair after she won the tournament. She's jumping up and down, pumping her fists in the air, as the crowd cheers.

"Ugh. Do I really sound like that?" She tugs on one of her braids. She ditched the blond and is back to black, aside from a skunk streak of deep purple. I'm proud of her for coming tonight and for making peace with Marisol and Avery. I know it wasn't easy. She's not over what happened—that will take longer than a week—but she's trying.

"Yes," Avery replies, smiling. She and Marisol are sitting on a couple of fold-up camping chairs Marisol's parents keep tucked in the storage under the stairs.

Violet makes a face at her.

"So, how did I get here? How did I, someone who had only played Catan a handful of times in my life, go on to beat nearly a hundred other people and win a seat at the Catan United States Championship?" Violet's voice rings out. "Well, to answer that, I guess I'll need to take you back to the beginning."

She freezes on the screen, mid-leap, a triumphant smile on her face, and then the footage slowly starts to rewind. The smile drops away; Violet sits back down in her chair; the cards fly back into her hands. The footage speeds up, faster and faster, until it finally stops on a shot of Violet and me at Bonus Round, the very first time I invited her to play Catan with us. I didn't realize that Alistair had even captured that moment.

"There's no way you picked the game up that quickly," on-screen Marisol says as Violet neatly arranges her orange game pieces.

Real-time Marisol wrinkles her nose. "Wait. I don't really sound like that, do I?"

"Yes, you do." Avery leans over and grabs her hand.

Violet's eyes never leave the screen, but from the way she crosses her arms, I know she's seen them. I wish Avery and Marisol would be a little more sensitive to her feelings, but I also know what it's like to be so into someone—how you reach for that person all the time because you're trying to reassure yourself that they're still there, that they're actually real and you haven't dreamed them up.

As Violet continues to narrate her journey to the Catan finals on-screen, I sneak a look at Alistair. This is also something I do a lot—stare at him. He's wearing a Van Halen T-shirt under a black vest, his dark curls falling into his eyes. He feels me looking at him and he turns away from the screen and smiles.

I reach into my hoodie pocket and my fingers brush against the yellow crystal. I've taken to carrying it with me, to remind myself just how lucky I am that I got a second chance with him—with all my friends.

I'm not a fortune-teller—obviously I can't predict what the future will hold for Alistair and me—but I do know that wherever life takes us, I'll always have these memories. Next year, when we're all scattered around the country, separated by thousands of miles and the excitement of college and new friends, when we've all moved on and are no longer part of one another's daily lives, I'll remember this moment.

Knowing there's not a thing that I would do differently.

✳ ACKNOWLEDGMENTS ✳

So many people have made my dream of writing books a reality. Thank you to my wonderful agent, Hannah Fergesen, for her support, creativity, and sage advice. Thank you to my amazing editor, Kat Brzozowski, and the entire Swoon Reads team, including Jean Feiwel, Lauren Scobell, Emily Settle, Morgan Rath, Karen Sherman, and Trisha Previte.

Thank you to Fernanda Viveiros, my publicist at Raincoast Books, and to all the librarians, bloggers, booksellers, and readers out there supporting and promoting books.

Thank you, as always, to my friends and family. I'm so lucky to have such a great circle of people around me, including: Erin Cassone, Mike and Tila Cassone, Chris and Carla Cassone, Dallas and Todd DePagie, Ray Dosanj and Harpreet Gill, Leiko Greaves, Sandy Hall, Brian and Joy Honeybourn, Barbara Hsiao, Mandy James, James and Elizabeth Koprich, Martin and Kathy Kania, Tracy Lundell, Shaun and Carianne McKay, Jennifer McKenzie, Pam and Russ Morrison, Stacie and Stavros Palivos, Karam and Varinder Rai, Nadine Silver, Jim and Jela Stanic, Robert Stanic and Ange Grim, Anna Tennick and Rickey Yada and Marg Timmins.

And thank you to Tony and Lila—the two brightest stars in my sky.

Check out more books
chosen for publication
by readers like you.

DID YOU KNOW...

readers like you
helped to get this
book published?

Join our book-obsessed community and help us
discover awesome new writing talent.

1

Write it.
Share your original YA manuscript.

2

Read it.
Discover bright new bookish talent.

3

Share it.
Discuss, rate, and share your faves.

4

Love it.
Help us publish the books you love.

Share your own manuscript or dive between the pages
at **swoonreads.com** or by downloading the **Swoon Reads app.**